The Return
Ken Sandoval

This is a work of fiction. Similarities to real people, places, or events are entirely coincidental.

THE RETURN

First edition. December 10, 2024.

Copyright © 2024 Ken Sandoval.

ISBN: 979-8230175964

Written by Ken Sandoval.

Also by Ken Sandoval

The Guardians
Crimson Harvest
Threads of Intrigue
The Return

Chapter 1

Dr. Jessica Middleton stared intently at the sample under her microscope. The deep-Earth mineral gleamed an iridescent purple, unlike anything Jessica had seen before. She adjusted the magnification, puzzling over the sample's unique crystalline structure.

As a leading xenoarchaeologist at the Planetary Science Institute, Jessica was accustomed to examining exotic geological samples. But this one, extracted from a borehole over six miles deep, was different. The mineral almost seemed engineered, hinting at some advanced technology far beyond human capabilities.

Jessica's concentration was broken by her lab assistant, Noah, bursting into the room. "Dr. Middleton, you need to see this!" he exclaimed. "Something massive just appeared over New York City!"

Jessica rushed with Noah to the institute's data center. On a large display, live news footage showed a mammoth alien spacecraft hovering over Manhattan. Around the world, similar ships were appearing above major cities. Stunned silence gripped the room.

Then pandemonium erupted. Phones rang incessantly as government officials scrambled for answers. Jessica stood frozen, struggling to process the revelation unfolding before her eyes. First contact with an extraterrestrial civilization had finally happened on a global scale.

Within hours, Jessica was boarding a military transport jet to New York City. The U.N. Security Council had requested her expertise given her background in xenoarchaeology and astrobiology. As humanity's first encounter with intelligent alien life, her insights would be crucial for understanding their origins and intentions.

Peering out the jet's window, Jessica took in the enormity of the cigar-shaped ship that now cast its shadow over the New York skyline. Smaller saucer-like vessels darted around it like pilot fish tending to a whale. What alien race was capable of constructing such colossal interstellar craft? And what did they want from humanity? Jessica's pulse quickened, both with exhilaration and apprehension.

The jet touched down at a U.N. airfield. Jessica and her military escort were whisked to the U.N. headquarters downtown. Security was on high alert, with checkpoints and vehicle inspections at every entrance. Inside the iconic Secretariat Building, delegates and translators filled the halls, abuzz with nervous speculation about the monumental events unfolding.

Jessica was shown to the Security Council chambers. Secretaries-General from five continents turned to greet her as she entered. "Dr. Middleton, thank you for coming on such short notice," said Secretary-General Gabriel Wellshire, extending his hand. "Please, have a seat."

Jessica settled into her chair facing a large video screen at the end of the conference table. Wellshire continued,

"Approximately two hours ago, we received this transmission from the alien vessels."

The screen flickered to life, displaying a humanoid alien seated against an iridescent background. Its skin was pale gray, with a bald, elongated skull and large oval eyes. When it spoke, its voice was melodic yet inhuman:

"Greetings. We are the Progenitors. We come in peace and wish to establish contact with the leadership of your world. We have traveled far to meet you, children of Earth."

Murmurs rippled around the table. Jessica studied the alien's unsettling features, her mind racing. The Secretary-General waited for the commotion to subside before continuing.

"We must proceed cautiously. Dr. Middleton, can you advise us? Do you believe their intentions are benign?"

Jessica chose her words carefully. "The lack of aggression is encouraging. But their capabilities are unknown. I recommend opening a dialogue to establish trust and learn their motives."

The Secretary-General nodded. "Then let us engage in this historic moment with hope and vigilance."

He opened a communication channel to the Progenitor ship. The same alien appeared, awaiting their response.

"Greetings. I am Secretary-General Gabriel Wellshire, representing the United Nations of Earth." Wellshire's voice was steady but solemn. "We wish to welcome you in the spirit of peace and cooperation. How shall we address you?"

The alien blinked its liquid black eyes. "I am Orius, Chief Science Envoy of our civilization. We have traveled far seeking those lost to us. Let us convene so that we may share what we know of your forgotten past."

Cryptic excitement rippled through the chamber. The Secretary-General proceeded cautiously.

"Very well. A delegation will meet with you at a secure location of your choosing."

Orius inclined his head. "We are sending coordinates. We look forward to communing with our lost children."

The transmission ended abruptly. Jessica felt a chill down her spine. The alien's words hinted at revelations that could upend humanity's understanding of itself. She steeled herself for the momentous discoveries to come.

Within the hour, Jessica was aboard a helicopter en route to a remote mountain valley, flanked by two Progenitor ships guiding them to the meeting point.

The helicopter touched down in a wide, rocky valley nestled between snow-capped peaks. Jessica stepped out into the cold mountain air, the thrum of rotor blades fading behind her. Before them stood Orius and two other aliens, clad in shimmering robes that contrasted starkly with the barren landscape. Hundreds of meters overhead, one of the colossal Progenitor ships loomed like a small moon fixed in place.

The Secretary-General approached, flanked by six U.N. delegates. Orius stepped forward and placed a closed fist over his chest.

"Greetings, Secretary-General. We welcome you in the spirit of unity." His voice was smooth and sonorous.

Wellshire mirrored the alien's gesture. "And we welcome you in a spirit of cooperation and discovery." He motioned to Jessica. "May I present Dr. Jessica Middleton, our chief advisor on xenoarchaeology and cross-cultural exchange."

Orius appraised Jessica with his fathomless eyes. "The one who interprets the relics of the past. A noble calling."

Jessica bowed slightly. "You honor me. I look forward to learning more about your civilization."

Orius bowed lower in return. "And we look forward to enlightening you about your own."

With pleasantries exchanged, they turned and entered a small Progenitor shuttle craft parked nearby. Crystalline control panels pulsed with pale light as Jessica took a seat beside the Secretary-General. She scrutinized the alien technology, utterly foreign to human science. What feats was it capable of?

The shuttle rose soundlessly, angling towards the massive ship overhead. Jessica gazed out the transparent hull, taking in the staggering scale of the alien vessel. Clusters of smaller craft darted around it like remoras tending a whale. She tried to imagine what alien world had produced such advanced technology.

They passed through a shimmering force field into a hangar bay large enough to swallow a city district. The air smelled strangely sterile, with a faint astringent taste. Gravity felt slightly weaker here, adding a subtle spring to Jessica's step. Alien constructs she could not begin to grasp filled the space.

Orius led them through a maze of corridors with gently pulsing walls. Some passages opened onto dizzying spaces crisscrossed by bridges wide enough for ten people abreast. Other aliens studied the delegation with quiet interest before returning to their inscrutable tasks. There was a hushed, temple-like air to the place.

Finally, they entered a grand, domed chamber with tiered seating rising along the walls. One entire side was open to space, highlighting the breathtaking curve of Earth. Jessica caught her breath at the spectacle.

Orius bade them to sit. "My friends, I understand you have many questions. We shall endeavor to answer them all in time. But first, allow us to share with you a wondrous truth."

He made a gesture, and the projected image of Earth swirled and transformed into a vista of otherworldly trees under a violet sky. "For generations, your people have gazed up at the stars and pondered the question...are we alone? Today we can definitively say the answer is no."

Holographic displays sprang to life, showing the progression of an alien civilization across countless worlds.

"We have traveled among the stars for longer than your civilizations have existed. We are but one of a vast, ancient community spanning the cosmos. And humanity is no mere newcomer to this community."

He fixed Jessica with an intense gaze. "Your people are the inheritors of a proud legacy, one forgotten but never lost. We have traveled far to reunite our estranged families."

Murmurs rippled through the delegates. The Secretary-General leaned forward. "What exactly do you mean? Does humanity share some connection with your people?"

Orius smiled cryptically. "All will be made clear." He stood. "Please, come with me."

He led them to an adjoining antechamber. In the center sat a waist-high pedestal topped with an oblong metallic case. Orius reverently opened it, bathing the room in pale blue light.

Nestled inside the case were rows of strange artifacts - figurines, tablets, crystalline shards.

"These relics were unearthed on your world by our survey teams. They bear markings unlike any human script." He lifted a small tablet, its surface etched with swirling alien symbols. "Yet our tests confirm the creators were Homo sapiens."

He let the statement sink in. Jessica's pulse raced as she examined the artifacts. Could humanity's roots truly extend into the stars?

Orius lifted a finger-length crystal rod that glimmered in the light. "This memory shard holds holographic records documenting Earth's settlement millennia ago. Early humans were brought here to mature spiritually and intellectually, after showing great promise."

"Brought here...by your people?" Jessica asked hesitantly.

Orius nodded. "Indeed. We call ourselves the Progenitors, for we seeded humanity on Earth, and many other worlds."

For a moment, silence gripped the entire assembly. Then excited questions burst forth as delegates crowded around the case, clamoring to inspect the artifacts. If confirmed, this revelation would shake human history to its very core. Jessica's mind reeled at the implications.

After months studying signals from the stars, had she underestimated just how profound this moment of first contact could be?

The clamor subsided as Secretary-General Wellshire raised his hands. "While astonishing, these claims require rigorous verification. Dr. Middleton, please examine the artifacts."

Jessica straightened, aware all eyes were on her. This was the purpose she had been called here for. Steeling her nerves, she activated her portable scanner and began sweeping the first object—a small crystalline tablet. The device mapped the intricate grooves across its surface, analyzing composition and age.

To her surprise, the tablet was over 60 million years old. Jessica took samples from three more items, each dating back impossibly far. The materials were familiar yet engineered with a complexity exceeding human technology. Her mind reeled at the implications.

Orius studied her carefully. "What have you found?"

Jessica took a breath. "The items are made of terrestrial compounds and do appear extremely ancient. But proving a definitive link to humanity requires more extensive testing."

The Secretary-General nodded. "We must continue with diligence and care. Dr. Middleton will continue analysis at our most advanced facilities." He turned to Orius. "Extraordinary claims require extraordinary evidence. Please grant us time to confirm what you've shown us."

The alien smiled diplomatically. "Of course. We shall provide further data to aid your analysis. Take whatever time is needed." He closed the artifact case and touched Jessica's shoulder. "The past beckons. Heed its call."

Jessica suppressed a shiver, unsure what to make of his cryptic words. The delegates prepared to leave, but she lingered, casting one last look over the sprawling alien metropolis outside. What other revelations lay in store? She was tempted to stay, to unravel the Progenitors' secrets. But caution overruled her curiosity.

Back on Earth, Jessica settled into a secure lab at U.N. headquarters, poring over the data from her scans. The evidence was puzzling, but inconclusive. She would need direct genetic testing to make a definitive link between the artifacts and humanity's origins.

Obtaining DNA would require a leap of trust by the Progenitors. Some factions were already pushing for it, hoping to accelerate revelations about humanity's past. Others urged caution, fearing the aliens had some hidden agenda. For now, the U.N. had agreed to temporary supervised visits by small groups of humans.

Jessica herself was divided. Her instincts told her the implications were too profound to rush. But the temptation to uncover the ultimate hidden truth about human history was powerful. She tried to focus on the methodical scientific steps ahead. The secrets of the past were beginning to stir but could not be unlocked overnight.

Outside her lab, the world was in upheaval. Wild theories and debates raged across the globe. Religious groups denounced the aliens as deceivers, while some embraced them as messiahs. World markets were seesawing violently amid the uncertainty.

For the first time in history, all of humanity was grappling with a shared revelation. And where it would lead was still impossible to grasp. The only certainty was that from this point on, Earth's place in the cosmos would never be the same.

Chapter 2

Two weeks after the Progenitors' arrival, Jessica found herself once again ascending to the alien mothership. This time, however, she was not alone—the Secretary-General and a full delegation of diplomats were accompanying her.

As their shuttle glided into the hangar bay, Jessica's eyes widened. They were greeted not just by Orius, but by a dozen Progenitors flanking a regal alien who was clearly their leader. His ornate robes cascaded to the floor, glittering with intricate geometric designs. The delegates stared in awe as he spread his arms in welcome.

"Greetings, valued guests. I am Valion, Chief Science Consul for our people. We are honored to receive the leaders of Earth."

Wellshire bowed respectfully. "The honor is ours. Please accept our gratitude for this historic opportunity."

Valion smiled benevolently. "Today, we shall share revelations about your planet and species, so that all intelligent life can thrive together."

He turned, his robes billowing as he led them onto the sprawling ship. Jessica walked alongside Orius through the maze of alien architecture. There was a reverent hush in the passageways, and everywhere crew members stepped aside and bowed as Valion passed.

Eventually they arrived at a circular chamber with a raised dais at the center. Valion took his place atop it and motioned for the delegates to sit nearby. With a wave of his hand, the dais projected a holographic image into the space above him—a slowly rotating model of DNA.

"The essence of life itself," Valion intoned. "Within every living cell resides the code of its genesis. Let us examine it."

The image zoomed onto the twisting ladder structure of the DNA. Valion glanced at Jessica. "Your scans of our artifacts were most illuminating. But genes reveal truths scans alone cannot."

Orius stepped forward, holding a small crystalline cylinder that glinted in the ambient light. "This contains genetic samples from our survey teams. If you provide human DNA for comparison, the connection shall be laid bare."

Jessica's pulse quickened. This was the moment of truth, when theory would give way to cold, hard facts. The Secretary-General turned to her and nodded. Taking a steadying breath, Jessica opened her field kit and drew out a sealed biopsy needle. She pricked her finger and let a drop of blood fall into a collecting capsule, then handed it to Orius.

"I offer this genetic sample, in trust and good faith."

Solemnly Orius pressed the two capsules into recesses in the alien projector. The hologram flickered, splitting into two DNA models and highlighting subtle variations between them. Jessica leaned forward intently, noting tiny but unmistakable similarities, like long-lost cousins rediscovering their kinship.

Valion nodded gravely. "There can no longer be doubt. Your people and mine share common genetic roots, stamped over eons into the very code of life."

For a moment, silence fell over the entire delegation as the weight of the revelation sunk in. Then excited chatter broke out among the diplomats. The Secretary-General stood slowly, visibly moved.

"You have given us definitive proof of a profound connection with your people. This forever alters humanity's understanding of itself. You have our deepest gratitude."

Valion spread his hands beneficently. "The truth belongs to all sapient beings. Let this be but the first step in a unified journey of discovery."

Jessica's mind was racing. Part of her had still clung to a slender hope that this had all been an elaborate deception. But with her own eyes she had witnessed science confirm the alien claims about humanity's genesis. As a seeker of knowledge, her world was expanding rapidly into terra incognita.

Orius approached her. "Your genetic signature is quite unique. Perhaps later you would consent to a more thorough examination?"

Jessica hesitated. More exhaustive testing could reveal further secrets, but the implications gave her pause. For now, there were bigger revelations to grapple with.

As the delegation made their farewells, Valion left them with an intriguing offer. "If any among you wish to journey further into these truths, we welcome visitors keen to explore our culture and worlds. Our doors are open to you."

Excited chatter broke out as they boarded the shuttle back to Earth. Humanity's understanding of itself would never again be the same.

In the weeks following the DNA revelations, the Progenitors' invitation sparked intense global debate. Some were eager to visit the alien ships, hungry for more revelations about humanity's past. But others saw risks, wanting to move slowly until the intentions of these powerful newcomers were clear.

Arguments raged late into the night at U.N. headquarters as delegates weighed the implications. In the end, they reached a compromise—a limited citizen exchange program would be started, allowing small, supervised groups of humans to briefly visit Progenitor vessels.

Strict screening criteria were established, selecting for scientific backgrounds and psychological stability. Jessica found herself on the review panel, poring over potential candidates. In the end, they selected an eclectic group of twelve, from biologists and anthropologists to engineers and linguists.

The day arrived for the first exchange. Jessica rode up with the delegates in a nervous silence. As their shuttle bayed through the shimmering force field, she could feel excitement and anxiety swirling within the group. She tried to reassure them but inwardly shared their trepidation. They were venturing into the unknown.

The Progenitors greeted them warmly, then split the group for specialized tours. Jessica was paired with a female alien named Sella, who had a Xeno-biologist's intense curiosity about human physiology and culture. Jessica deflected her endless delicate questions as best she could while taking in the strange sights around her.

Some of the other delegates later reported feeling their Progenitor hosts were closely scrutinizing them for minute reactions during their tours. Jessica had noticed the same subtle sense of being observed in her own group. It reinforced her feeling that, despite outward friendliness, the aliens had their own undisclosed agenda.

The most memorable moment came near the end, when Sella brought Jessica onto a long observation deck overlooking an alien sea. Three moons hung against a glittering nebula backdrop, bathing everything in a haunting indigo light. Despite nagging doubts, Jessica was struck by the beauty of this glimpse beyond Earth. For better or worse, the universe had become far larger.

After returning home, Jessica got to work analyzing volumes of data collected by the group. Alien technology was far beyond human science, making insight difficult. But there were patterns, subtle clues about the Progenitors' goals and history. She was downloading Raman spectra when her colleague Noah rushed into the lab, his face pale.

"Jessica, you need to see this. It's spreading all over the net."

She followed him to the lounge, where a crowd had gathered around the wall screen. Her heart sank as footage played of violence erupting during protests across the globe. Many were demonstrating against what they saw as a conspiracy to undermine humanity's origins on Earth. The exchanges had inflamed tensions rather than easing them.

Jessica watched grimly with the others, knowing this chaos was only the beginning of a historic upheaval in human self-understanding. With a heavy feeling she returned to her lab, wondering if she had helped set in motion something no one would be able to control.

Over the next few weeks, anti-alien sentiment continued festering in segments of the population. Jessica's colleague Dr. James Wright was sympathetic to the protestors' skepticism.

"Healthy caution is wise with powers greater than ours," he told Jessica over lunch one day. "We embraced nuclear science too hastily once."

Jessica valued his perspective as a xenobiology expert on her team. But privately she felt he was being overcautious. Progress always came with risks.

Travel to the motherships continued, but under tighter security. Jessica helped debrief the returning delegates, pressing them for insights on Progenitor culture and technology. Most described an advanced but stagnant society, with rigid traditions and social structure. Their science seemed focused on decoding biology and consciousness.

One exchange participant, a cyberneticist named Ada Zhang, noticed the Progenitors avoided queries about their homeworlds. "When I asked where their civilization began, they changed the subject. It felt...evasive."

Jessica found this odd. Perhaps they had environmental collapse or resource scarcity they wished to hide. She made a mental note to dig deeper into their history.

Late one evening, Jessica was alone analyzing Progenitor crystal samples when the lab doors opened. She looked up, surprised to see Secretary Wellshire enter. He approached her workspace, his expression grim.

"Dr. Middleton, my apologies for the late hour. There is a sensitive matter I wanted to discuss discreetly. We have discovered...discrepancies in the Progenitors' accounts of human history."

Jessica's fatigue vanished. "What discrepancies?"

"Problems with the dating of ancient sites they helped uncover. Several appear much younger than they claim. And genetic data from you and the delegates suggests their connection to humanity is..." He searched for the word. "...exaggerated."

Jessica's mind raced. "Evidence of deception?"

"Unclear. We cannot rule out errors from our own limited science." Wellshire sighed. "For now, we must quietly investigate without rousing suspicion."

Jessica nodded. "I will analyze the data thoroughly."

After Wellshire left, she sat thinking hard. If the Secretary-General's suspicions proved true, humanity could be dealing with a cosmic agenda it did not understand. She would have to be extremely careful in her work moving forward. The truth about the past was never as simple as it seemed.

Jessica spent the next few days combing through historical and genetic data related to the Progenitors' claims, searching for any evidence of fabrication or manipulation. The records they had provided showed human habitation of sites across the globe dating back over 60 million years. But when she carbon dated soil samples from the sites in the lab, the results were far more recent—within the last 10,000 years. A stark and troubling discrepancy.

Similarly, analysis of her own genetic samples alongside the Progenitors' revealed commonalities consistent with shared mammalian descent hundreds of millions of years ago. But distinct markers specific to Homo sapiens only appeared in the human genome during the evolutionary period accepted by human science. The purported direct seeding by the Progenitors was nowhere to be found.

The evidence was showing the Progenitors had exaggerated, if not outright fabricated, key elements of humanity's genetic heritage and presence on Earth. But why attempt such an elaborate deception? What was their true agenda? Jessica could only guess.

She reported her confidential findings to Secretary Wellshire. He concurred with her assessment, his expression grim. "This casts their motives in a concerning light," he said. "For now, we cannot reveal this knowledge more widely. Discretion is essential while we figure out how to respond."

Jessica understood his need for secrecy, but keeping such explosive discoveries quiet would be challenging. She tightened data protections in her lab and leaked altered findings with fabricated results supporting the Progenitors' claims. It was a stopgap measure at best. Word was already spreading among delegations that not all was as it seemed.

The implications weighed on Jessica as she left the U.N. building late one evening. On impulse, she decided to take a longer route home through the city. As she strolled past a park, something peculiar caught her eye – a slim hooded figure standing half-concealed behind a tree, seemingly watching the U.N. complex. As Jessica stared, the figure turned abruptly and melted into the night.

Unease trickled through her. Secretary Wellshire was right to be cautious. Dangerous currents swirled beneath the surface of historic events now set in motion. And Jessica suspected her own role was far from over.

Chapter 3

In the pre-dawn hours, Jessica sat alone in her office, contemplating her next steps. The discrepancies she'd uncovered had confirmed the Secretary-General's fears—the Progenitors were hiding something about humanity's past. But what, and why? She needed more information.

A message popped up on her screen—an encrypted communication from Wellshire. It contained coordinates for a secure meeting later that morning. Jessica acknowledged the message, then began drafting a summary of her confidential findings to share with him. She also put together a list of potential ways to discreetly uncover more about the Progenitors' agenda.

At the specified time, Jessica arrived at the coordinates, an anonymous office complex outside the city. She was ushered into a sparsely furnished meeting room where Wellshire and two senior advisors were already waiting.

"Thank you for coming, Dr. Middleton," Wellshire said. "I know you're taking a substantial risk. Rest assured we shall guard your contribution closely."

Jessica slid her summary document across the table. "Here are my conclusions based on the data available so far. I have concerns about the Progenitors' accounts of our past."

Wellshire reviewed her report with a furrowed brow while his advisors looked on grimly. "This substantiates our own misgivings," he said. "You believe their claims were exaggerated?"

"Possibly fabricated entirely," Jessica said. "Though proving intent would require more evidence."

"Which we must obtain, without revealing our doubts," Wellshire mused. "A delicate game of strategy begins. What approaches do you suggest?"

Jessica presented her proposals: covert scans of Progenitor databases, intelligence gathering in their delegations, and cultivating skeptical insiders among their researchers. Each method had merits and risks.

After much debate, Wellshire decided their priority must be protectively limiting the Progenitors' access to human society while discreetly probing their intentions. He would share Jessica's findings with only their most trusted advisors. "This knowledge must be safeguarded for now," he told her gravely. "Much is at stake."

Over the next week, Jessica saw the effects of Wellshire's strategy. Progenitor visitation programs were scaled back due to "logistical problems." Several planned student cultural exchanges were quietly canceled. Only strictly supervised delegations continued between their ship and U.N. headquarters.

Meanwhile, Jessica helped recruit human researchers who were unsettled by discrepancies in the Progenitors' accounts and willing to covertly aid the investigation. One volcanologist named Kenji Takahashi had noticed surprising activity around seismic anomalies the aliens claimed were ancient sites. His account gave Jessica hope they could unravel the truth.

But secrecy weighed on her. She knew the public would eventually demand full disclosure. Wellshire hoped to control the timing, but anticipation was building. Rumored leaks were already spreading theories ranging from the Progenitors secretly harvesting organics to enslaving humans for labor. Speculation was outpacing truth.

That evening, exiting her lab, Jessica noticed two men visibly watching the building's entrance. A third lurked near a parked van, trying to look casual. Jessica's pulse quickened. She had seen enough surveillance to recognize it. The situation was ominous.

As she hurried towards home, she couldn't shake the feeling hidden forces were now in motion, and any misstep could bring them crashing down on her. She would need to be very careful. Much more than her career was at risk.

Jessica felt increasingly like she was being watched. On her commute, at the grocery store, even walking in the park, the same few suspicious faces would reappear. She tried altering her routine, taking different routes to shake any followers. But the lingering eyes persisted.

Clearly, word of her classified discoveries was spreading. But who was showing this interest? Foreign intelligence services? Private extremist groups? Jessica could only speculate.

At the lab, she discreetly re-examined samples that the Progenitors claimed proved an ancient human settlement. The site was supposedly over 50 million years old, long predating human evolution. But radiometric dating of the same shale samples on her equipment showed they were barely 50 thousand years old. Another falsehood was revealed.

Jessica reported her findings via encrypted message to Secretary Wellshire. His reply was blunt: "Say nothing. Will send a security team."

That evening, two agents met Jessica at her apartment to discreetly escort her to a safehouse. She packed quickly, hands trembling slightly as she grabbed essentials. Was she overreacting? Or was the threat real? There was no time to wonder.

At the nondescript safehouse, the gravity of her situation sank in. She was now a security liability, requiring protection. And she still didn't fully grasp why.

A few hours later, Wellshire himself arrived, his expression weary and stressed. Jessica quickly asked, "What do we know? Who is after this information?"

The Secretary-General shook his head. "As yet, unclear. We have heard whispers of several fringe groups aggressively seeking any dirt that discredits the Progenitors. But their true motivations and resources are still unknown."

He sighed. "What matters now is keeping you and your knowledge protected. Your findings have made you dangerously conspicuous."

Jessica nodded uneasily. She had tried honoring the ethic of science by following evidence wherever it led. But those very principles now made her a target. The integrity she valued so highly had pushed her to this precipice. Where it led from here was frighteningly uncertain.

She avoided the windows, wary of who might be lurking outside. Until answers emerged, she was trapped in this limbo, cut off from her work and watched by obscure forces she could not see or name. The secrets she had unearthed were no longer buried.

Jessica waited anxiously for updates from Wellshire's team. She missed the purposeful bustle of her lab and the ability to actively investigate the mounting questions about the Progenitors. But she understood the need for caution. There were hidden players with unknown motives lurking in the shadows, and any rash move could prove dangerous.

Occasional encrypted messages provided updates. Wellshire's advisors were apparently pursuing backchannel inquiries and monitoring chatter in various dark corners of the net. One message informed her that several fringe groups had demonstrated surprising resources to mobilize and spread anti-Progenitor narratives aligned with her findings.

One shadowy European nationalist organization had recruited scientists to re-analyze the alien data, concluding the Progenitors had nefarious intentions. An American libertarian group decried the extraterrestrials as collectivist conquerors aiming to subordinate humanity. The often contradictory theories had one common thread: justifying hostility toward the newly arrived aliens.

Jessica noted with unease the emerging patterns of fear mongering. Sensational claims spread faster than nuance, inflaming tensions. She could easily envision demagogues hijacking this climate of uncertainty to stoke alienation and division for their own disruptive ends. But without the full facts, her power to counteract this was limited.

Eight tense days passed before Wellshire himself paid an unexpected visit. Jessica pressed him eagerly for any leads on who was tracking her research, but he shook his head. "It appears to be a loose coalition of various entities. Isolating one is difficult." His expression turned graver. "Misinformation is spreading rapidly surrounding your work. We can't contain it."

Jessica's heart sank. "So where does this leave us? The truth will come out, but fragmented and distorted?"

"I'm afraid so," Wellshire said. "Your findings have taken on a life of their own. Containing them is impossible now." He stood and paced, looking uncharacteristically defeated.

"The wisest course I can see is a gradual release of evidence on our terms, to get ahead of sensational rumors. Perhaps paired with restricted transparency measures for the Progenitors to ease tensions."

He turned back to Jessica. "It is now a delicate dance to reveal the complex truth responsibly, neither concealing facts nor inflaming hysteria. I hope you can resume your research soon to aid our efforts."

Jessica felt the burden of her inadvertent role in escalating global tensions swirling around the aliens. But she still believed science and reason offered the surest path ahead. "I am ready to continue the investigation," she told Wellshire with as much confidence as she could summon. "Knowledge remains our sharpest tool against fear and deception."

In her heart, though, doubts lingered. Forces were in motion now far beyond her control. Where they would lead humanity and its place in the universe remained frighteningly unclear. She could only follow her principles and hope that ethics and empathy would guide her forward through these difficult times.

Jessica worked closely with Wellshire's team to plan their strategy for controlled disclosure. Their priorities were isolating key evidence that definitively contradicted the Progenitors' accounts, while avoiding fueling dangerous speculation.

For the gradual evidence release, Jessica recommended they focus on radiometric dating of supposed ancient sites the aliens had highlighted. The samples definitively placed the origins of those sites within the period accepted by human archaeology, not millions of years ago as claimed. She also suggested emphasizing the lack of any distinct genetic markers shared only by humans and Progenitors, which undercut their assertions about directly seeding humanity.

To get the Progenitors involved in transparency, Wellshire proposed they invite alien leaders to take part in jointly led scientific expeditions at disputed sites. This could allow humans to monitor their reactions closely while demonstrating cooperation. Jessica added they should push for exchanges of junior researchers to foster greater trust.

On tracking misinformation, they decided a priority was checking online group chatter to find conspiracy theories and doctored evidence spreading virally. Jessica also recommended deep analysis of data traffic and web archives to uncover potential hidden coordination driving malicious disinformation campaigns.

"Comprehensive fact-finding is crucial," Wellshire emphasized. "We must understand the roots of this climate of fear before countering it responsibly."

Jessica acknowledged the value in his methodical approach. They were walking a fine line between responding decisively and acting recklessly without fully grasping complex truths. If wisdom and ethics were to prevail, they needed knowledge that penetrated deeper than headlines and patriotism.

In her heart, Jessica still believed humanity could manage even painful truths with resilience, as long as they were illuminated by principles of science and compassion. But powerful forces now strained that faith. Their methods had to be as enlightened as the ideals they hoped to uphold.

As Wellshire's team completed plans to involve the Progenitors in transparency measures, Jessica considered potential complications. The aliens had already shown a willingness to bend the truth to their agenda. Closely watching them was crucial.

She proposed they structure joint expeditions so the Progenitors could not limit human access to disputed sites. Independent verification was vital. They also needed to press for equal transparency into alleged Progenitor settlements on Earth to build trust.

Regarding public communication, Jessica recommended gradually presenting the contradictions in the aliens' accounts through experts who could add context and caution. Blunt government proclamations risked feeding conspiracy theories. Layered academic analysis would lend credibility.

Wellshire agreed, noting they should recruit diverse scientific voices to avoid any hints of selectivity. "The message must clearly emerge from the consensus of empirical scrutiny, not imposed authority," he said.

Checking viral misinformation online, Jessica highlighted social media's role as a rumor mill. She suggested covertly seeding bogus rumors on fringe platforms to track how they mutated and spread. Network analysis could then find influential profiles boosting fabricated narratives so their reach could be curtailed.

"We must illuminate the shadows where decontextualized bits of data coalesce into dangerous disinformation," she told Wellshire. "Methodical cross-platform tracking is vital."

He concurred, and his tech team began work on a virtual web crawler to trace the growing tangle of claims surrounding the Progenitors across forums, video sites and social networks. Their goal was surgically excising malignant bits of misinformation before they metastasized across the global infosphere.

As Jessica studied their tracking system, she hoped its insights could map a path through this wilderness of mirrors where truth was so easily distorted. But she knew even the wisest plans would collide with volatile psychology and politics. If reason was to prevail, empathy would need to guide it.

Chapter 4

Two months after the Progenitors' arrival, Jessica stepped back into her lab, finally resuming her clandestine investigation. Despite lingering tensions swirling outside, it felt reassuring to be anchored again in the routine of research. She hoped science could still illuminate a way forward, if pursued responsibly.

She was reviewing the latest carbon dating results on alleged ancient sites when her lab door opened. Jessica looked up in surprise to see a tall, bald Progenitor entering. His intense green eyes locked onto hers.

"Dr. Middleton, I presume? I am Vorlus, Chief Science Consul for our expedition." He extended a long-fingered hand in greeting.

Jessica hesitated before shaking it. "You have me at a disadvantage. I was not informed of any visit."

Vorlus smiled disarmingly. "I wished to make your acquaintance informally. Our leaders speak highly of your...intellectual rigor." He gestured at her samples. "I see you waste no time resuming important work."

His compliment seemed polite, but something in his manner set Jessica on edge. She opted for neutral courtesy.

"Merely following where evidence leads. Scientific truth belongs to us all."

Vorlus nodded. "Indeed. In that spirit, might I examine your carbon dating data myself?"

Jessica tensed. Declining his request risked antagonizing a senior Progenitor. But she could not reveal her confidential findings.

She forced a smile. "I would be happy to share results once finalized and reviewed." Changing the subject, she asked, "How are you finding interactions with our people so far?"

Vorlus waved off the question airily. "Oh, most edifying. But it is the past that holds real intrigue, yes? The genesis of civilizations?"

He gazed around the lab, scrutinizing Jessica's equipment. She folded her arms, grateful that all sensitive data was strictly secured.

Finally, Vorlus sighed. "Well, I have trespassed on your time long enough. I look forward to our two peoples analyzing the ancient past together."

After he left, Jessica realized she had been holding her breath. Something about the Progenitor's manner left her deeply unsettled. She would definitely need to keep her guard up in these supposedly cooperative ventures. Not all their visitors' motives were transparent.

Following Vorlus' unexpected visit, Jessica took extra precautions with her ongoing investigation. She restricted lab access, enabled remote data wiping on devices, and set up decoy backup drives. It was possible the Progenitor science consul had simply been making introductory overtures, but his probing questions seemed calculated. Until she understood his motives, vigilance was key.

Jessica reached out to colleagues at other labs analyzing Progenitor data, subtly inquiring if they had received any recent alien visitors. Several reported similar unannounced calls by Vorlus asking probing questions about their research. He seemed particularly focused on geological and archaeological teams contradicting Progenitor accounts of human history.

Clearly, he was gathering intelligence, trying to assess how widely human scientists doubted the official narrative. Jessica informed Wellshire, who shared her concern and said he would raise the matter delicately with Progenitor leadership. They could not accuse Vorlus directly without evidence, but discreetly discouraging such unilateral visits seemed prudent.

Meanwhile, Jessica focused on shoring up the investigation's core scientific case. She re-examined key ancient sites highlighted by the Progenitors and ran more dating analyses using multiple methods. The results all converged—the origin times fell squarely within the accepted human chronology, not millions of years earlier as claimed. She compiled the multiple verification proofs into a confidential report for Wellshire.

While analyzing results late one night, Jessica noticed something peculiar in the sediment layers of samples from a dig site in Mongolia. There appeared to be signs of tampering, subtle but unmistakable to a trained eye. Her pulse quickened. This provided the first direct evidence that data had been actively fabricated.

Jessica prepared a separate encrypted file detailing her findings. This was a watershed development; incontrovertible proof the Progenitors had deliberately manipulated critical site data they provided. She did not yet know why, but with this evidence, confronting them directly was becoming inevitable. The truth could only stay buried for so long before its inconsistencies would be laid bare under the pitiless light of science.

Jessica scheduled an urgent meeting with Wellshire to present her evidence of data manipulation at the Mongolian site. This confirmation of deliberate falsification fundamentally changed the calculus of their investigation. Confrontation now seemed inevitable, though the risks were substantial.

Wellshire listened silently as she explained the tampering signs and possible methods used. His expression grew increasingly grave.

"This leaves little doubt about willful deception," he said when she had finished. "The question is why falsify this particular site. What are they obscuring?"

Jessica could only guess. Perhaps the Mongolian site held clues about ancient civilizations predating humanity's rise. Or its geology contradicted the Progenitors' account of continents and oceans in eras they claimed to have visited Earth. For now, their motives remained murky.

"We must secure any untainted samples from that site and conduct a full forensic analysis," Wellshire decided. "I will work with our allies in the Mongolian government to obtain access without arousing suspicion."

While Wellshire initiated diplomatic overtures, Jessica focused on tightening lab security. She restricted keycard access, installed network firewalls, and set up protocols for remote purging of drives. Vorlus' clandestine visit had shown the Progenitors were probing for vulnerabilities. She could not be too cautious.

A few days later, two unassuming containers arrived from Mongolia, transported via a trusted courier. Jessica secured the samples and got straight to work scrutinizing them. She scanned mineral composition, tested sediment particle size, analyzed microfossils—every test she could think of to extract clues. Late into the night, she pored over results, searching for any anomalies.

Her diligence was rewarded when she examined sediment deposition patterns. They held signs of unusual intermixing from multiple eras that natural causes alone could not explain. This deposit history was inconsistent with the site's supposed age. The Progenitors' deception ran deeper than she had realized.

Wellshire's response was sober when she reported her findings. "Now we have them," he said. "Such evidence will be difficult to explain away innocently."

He stood silently for a while, considering the implications. "Confrontation grows inescapable. We must plan our next steps very deliberately."

Jessica understood his caution. They were venturing into dangerous territory, politically and socially. But truth could not stay buried forever.

"The charade is unraveling," she said. "We must stay ahead of fear with facts. I can keep digging, discreetly."

Wellshire nodded slowly. "So be it. Your work is still critical. The light you shine may yet guide us through this darkness."

Though anxious about what lay ahead, Jessica returned to the lab with renewed purpose. She would follow the science relentlessly, wherever it led. Truth was their surest defense against chaos.

Having exposed data tampering by the Progenitors, Jessica focused on forensic analyses that could strengthen the evidence. She prioritized scrutinizing mineral composition and crystal lattice defects that could reveal inconsistencies with the site's supposed age. Isotopic dating of rare earth elements also had potential to expose fabrication.

To ensure her team's safety, Jessica instituted protocols limiting communication about the investigation. She secured sensitive data under lock and key, restricting access to those directly involved. Regular sweeps were conducted for tracking devices or surveillance equipment. Risks remained, but diligence could reduce them.

For potential allies, Wellshire discreetly reached out to figures in the scientific community and technology sphere who had openly questioned the Progenitors' motives. Several influential researchers and Silicon Valley leaders pledged support, offering resources to aid the inquiry. Wellshire also contacted trusted political counterparts in Russia and China to brief them, hoping to avoid geopolitical wildcards.

Jessica continued analyzing the Mongolian samples, working with geologists to model patterns of erosion and mountain formation around the excavation site. Their simulations suggested a far more recent chronology than the Progenitors kept.

Meanwhile, Wellshire's team was monitoring intelligence chatter closely. Rumors were circulating of shadowy Progenitor operatives recruiting fringe human groups to their cause through undisclosed incentives. If true, it raised concerns about infiltration and influence attempts.

"We must build our coalition carefully," Wellshire told Jessica. "Not all who offer friendship have pure motives. But there are those who value truth over power."

Jessica took his advice to heart. While she focused on the science, Wellshire strengthened relationships behind the scenes with principled allies—scientific, political and public. Their cautions inquiry was shedding light deeper into a past shrouded in shadows. But navigating the unseen currents ahead would require wisdom and trust in equal measure.

Jessica spent the next week immersed in testing the Mongolian samples, pushing the analysis to its limits. She worked late into each night, scrutinizing mineral composition and geochemical data from multiple angles, searching for any revelations. This site held answers; she could feel it.

Her efforts paid off one evening when examining rare earth element levels in sediment deposits. They followed a pattern over time that did not fit with the supposed age of the excavation site. The only plausible explanation was that the layers had been artificially mixed from different eras to create a veneer of antiquity.

Jessica summarized the results in a report titled simply "Indisputable Fraud." She double encrypted the file and sent it to Secretary Wellshire for review. His reply arrived within the hour: "This leaves no room for innocent explanations. We can't ignore such deception. Meet me at the location below in twelve hours."

The coordinates led to a nondescript warehouse on the city outskirts. Inside, Wellshire and two senior officials were waiting. Jessica handed over a copy of the forensic report. "The science leaves little doubt now. They doctored the data."

Wellshire nodded grimly. "Then it is time we arranged a formal meeting and presented this evidence. The charade has gone on long enough." He turned to his advisors. "I want all our supporting research and documentation prepared to transmit to the Progenitor leadership within 48 hours."

"That's a bold move," Jessica said uneasily. "How do you think they will respond?"

"With more falsehoods and deflections, I suspect," Wellshire said. "But we must persistently confront them with the truth. They underestimate human tenacity."

Jessica spent the next two days compiling and triple checking the investigation's exhaustive supporting data. This would be their definitive case laying bare the Progenitor deceptions and demanding accountability. The stakes made her nervous, but there was no turning back now.

The morning of the presentation, Jessica dressed in an understated but sharp pantsuit, wanting to project professionalism and authority. This would likely be a defining moment, for her personally and humanity as a whole.

At the U.N., security was on high alert. Jessica was ushered into the secretariat chamber along with Wellshire and his advisors. A delegation of Progenitor diplomats entered and took seats across from them. Jessica drew a deep breath. There was no more time for doubt or second guessing. She began to speak.

Jessica looked right at the Progenitor diplomats as she spoke.

"We've done extensive tests on the samples from the excavation site in Mongolia. The results make it clear the data was faked. Mineral levels from different time periods were mixed together. It seems you tried to make an old site look way older than it really is."

The Progenitors looked around at each other with worried expressions. One of them, named Vorlus, responded.

"There must be some mistake. We provided that data in good faith. It matched our historical records."

Jessica shook her head. "The science doesn't lie. Our tests checked out multiple ways. The samples were tampered with. We want to know why."

The Progenitors murmured amongst themselves. After a minute, their leader Gorhan spoke up.

"This is...concerning. We will look into it immediately. If errors were made, you have our deepest apologies."

But Secretary Wellshire didn't look convinced. "This wasn't a single error. Many sites you claimed were ancient turned out to be far more recent. It seems you have misled us about human history in ways we don't yet understand."

Gorhan spread his long hands. "Please, let us re-examine our archives. In time, I am sure we can resolve this confusion."

Jessica shook her head firmly. "We need answers and transparency now. The days of partial truths are over. What are you hiding about our past?"

The Progenitors looked between each other nervously. Finally, Gorhan sighed.

"Very well. It seems we have no choice now but to reveal the whole truth."

He nodded to Vorlus, who dimmed the lights and turned on a display screen.

"The story we must tell you stretches back over two hundred thousand years," he began.

Jessica listened intently, sensing everything was about to change.

Chapter 5

Jessica took a deep breath as Vorlus prepared to reveal the full history the Progenitors had been concealing. She steadied herself, knowing their story would likely challenge much of what humanity believed about its own origins and antiquity. But she was ready to listen with an open and discerning mind.

Vorlus activated a holographic display showing a vast galaxy. "Our two species' histories are intertwined, across vast eras and lightyears. To understand, we must start long ago and far away, on our ancient homeworld."

The display zoomed in on a small, dim planet orbiting a red dwarf star. "Here is where our civilization was born, over one million years ago. We evolved rapidly, developing interstellar travel within a few millennia."

The conference room filled with stunned murmurs. That timeline surpassed humanity's advancement by orders of magnitude.

Vorlus continued. "We discovered this galaxy and mapped thousands of worlds. Then, we encountered a planet of particular promise."

The hologram zoomed toward the Milky Way, stopping on an image of ancient Earth. "We call this planet Galia. It held an incredibly diverse and robust life. So, we made it a keystone of our explorations."

Jessica's mind reeled. Galia? Was that what the Progenitors called Earth across the eons? What did it imply about their interest in humanity's world? She shared an uneasy glance with Wellshire. There were revelations here beyond even their gravest suspicions.

Vorlus solemnly went on. "Galia has always been central to our interstellar journeys. But never as central or consequential, as in the era that changed the fates of both our species forever."

"Over two hundred thousand years ago, your world entered an ice age," Vorlus explained. "Galia's diverse life was under grave threat. We felt compelled to prevent a massive extinction."

He displayed images of the Progenitors terraforming ancient Earth, altering oceans and atmosphere. "We took bold action to stabilize Galia's climate, ensuring species survival."

Jessica was shocked. She exchanged stunned looks with Wellshire. The Progenitors had reshaped Earth's environment eons ago? The implications were staggering.

"Part of that effort involved cultivating fledgling intelligences we discovered, so they might one day aid Galia's stewardship." More images followed of Progenitors visiting primitive human tribes, providing tools and knowledge.

"We nurtured humanity, believing your potential was great. But then..." Vorlus hesitated. "Our actions had unforeseen consequences."

The display showed the Progenitors' homeworld, now barren and lifeless. "In focusing so much on Galia, we neglected our own planet. Its slow demise went unnoticed until it was too late. We sacrificed our cradle for one adopted."

Jessica felt pity stir unexpectedly. "Your entire world paid the price for trying to save Earth?"

Vorlus nodded solemnly. "We became refugees, wanderers between stars. Galia became more than a colony and our hopes rested in humanity fulfilling a duty we could not."

A heavy silence fell. Jessica's mind reeled. This revelation cast the Progenitors' interest in her world in a profoundly tragic light. They were bound to ancient Earth by more than origins, but by redemption. She glanced at Wellshire and knew they would need to process this humbly and with care.

"We taught your ancestors how to farm the land efficiently," Vorlus explained. "How to harvest seeds at the right times, divert rivers into irrigation, fertilize soil for bountiful crops."

Images displayed early humans learning agricultural techniques from patient Progenitor instructors.

"We also shared principles of medicine, engineering, and astronomy. The foundations that allowed your civilizations to thrive."

Jessica nodded slowly. "So much of our ancient knowledge originated with you."

Vorlus' expression became solemn. "As our homeworld declined, we devoted more attention to guiding humanity's rise. Perhaps too much."

The display showed magnificent Progenitor cities crumbling into ruin. "In neglecting our own world, we placed a heavy burden on your species. One you did not seek."

He sighed deeply. "And in impatience and arrogance, we made grave mistakes. We came to overestimate humanity's capabilities, expecting too much progress. When your societies fell short, our disdain grew."

The images turned dark, showing Progenitors looking down harshly on struggling humans.

The holograms showed Progenitors installing strange devices in human villages, seeming to manipulate brain activity. "We used technology to accelerate your ancestors' advancement, hoping to make you fitting stewards."

"Some leaders argued humanity should be left to grow naturally," Vorlus admitted. "But impatience won out. We presumed we knew best what course your species should take."

The results were not what the Progenitors intended. More images showed accelerated human societies collapsing into chaos and war. "The civilizations we forced along too rapidly crumbled under the strain. Your cultures needed room to develop at their own pace."

"We learned the dangers of arrogance. And the naivete of believing any species can simply stand in for another." Vorlus gave Jessica an apologetic look. "You deserved understanding and compassion. Often, we failed to provide it."

A complex swirl of emotions filled Jessica's heart. There was much to process in the wake of these profound revelations. But of one thing she felt certain, both their peoples could emerge wiser, with empathy and forgiveness lighting the way.

Jessica's mind raced as she tried to process the implications of the Progenitors' stunning revelations about their deep history with humanity. This enormous span of time encompassed the entire arc of human civilization and evolution. The Progenitors had been quietly present across countless generations, shaping the course of human development in ways that were only now coming to light. She glanced at Secretary Wellshire and saw her own shock mirrored in his eyes. They were navigating uncharted waters.

Vorlus gave them a moment to absorb his words before continuing. "After the decline of our homeworld, Galia became more than just a colony to us, it represented the future of our civilization. We placed immense pressure on humanity to follow the path of progress we set out."

Vorlus shook his head ruefully. "Our arrogance was our downfall. And it planted seeds of resentment towards us that lingered in humanity's memory over generations." The holograms showed Progenitors being driven away angrily by mobs of humans.

"We learned difficult lessons about the perils of presumption," Vorlus said. "And about respecting each species' right to self-determination. We retreated to the shadows to observe your more organic progress."

Jessica felt a mix of anger at the Progenitors' trespassing and curiosity about how it shaped human thought. She exchanged a look with Wellshire; they were thinking the same thing. There was much yet to unravel.

Vorlus solemnly concluded his story. "Now you understand our complex role in your history. We sought connection but created division. It is time to heal this rift with honesty and make amends through cooperation. We present your people with the gift of truth, difficult though it may be to receive."

He dimmed the holograms, leaving Jessica with racing thoughts and a multitude of questions. But she also felt the first stirrings of possibility. If both species could approach this fraught past with openness, perhaps they could build a new foundation of mutual understanding. It would require extraordinary wisdom and care. She only hoped they were ready for the challenge ahead. There was so much difficult work yet to be done.

Jessica sat in stunned silence, struggling to process the revelations Vorlus had laid out. Her mind reeled at the size of it all. The Progenitors had been present across the entire arc of human history, subtly influencing the course of civilization. It was almost too much to comprehend.

Glancing around the room, she saw similar reactions on the faces of Secretary Wellshire and the other human representatives. Some looked outraged, others fearful. A low murmur of anxious voices filled the air.

Across from them, the Progenitors sat solemnly with downcast eyes. Vorlus had shut off the holograms, but the images still haunted Jessica's mind. She flashed back to one of the ancient humans angrily driving the Progenitors away after their meddling caused a civilization's collapse. That resentment and distrust seemed to linger still in the tense air that now hung between the two delegations.

Vorlus broke the uncomfortable silence. "I know this is difficult to hear. But only with honesty can our peoples find reconciliation." His tone was conciliatory, but his words only echoed in Jessica's turbulent mind.

Secretary Wellshire slowly shook his head. He looked profoundly shaken, like a man who thought he knew the shape of the world only to have that foundation cracked open. When he finally spoke, his voice was hoarse with emotion.

"You presume much to tell us our history is a lie, then ask for trust." He paused and took a long, deep breath before continuing. "But the fault is not yours alone. We must all reflect deeply on what role our own fears and biases play in this rift."

Jessica felt her anger dissipate at Wellshire's thoughtful words. A fragile hope took root that compassion and openness could pave the way forward out of this situation if both sides had courage to face it together.

A heavy silence followed Wellshire's words as both groups sat with the weight of the revelations. Jessica's mind was still racing, trying to understand the scale of the Progenitors' involvement in human history. They had nurtured humanity's development like caretakers tending a garden. But in their hubris, they had also overstepped natural boundaries.

Jessica wondered how many other ancient civilizations might have been subtly shaped by the Progenitors in ways lost to time. How many pieces of the human story did not originate on Earth at all, but traveled between stars from an alien homeworld? It was a profound and deeply unsettling thought.

She studied the faces of the Progenitors, who looked back at her with solemn expressions. For all their advanced technology and wisdom, they were fallible gods, but imperfect beings who made grave mistakes. And carried immense regret. Jessica felt a wave of empathy for the heavy burden of their actions they still shouldered.

Secretary Wellshire slowly rose to address the Progenitors. "We can't change the past," he said quietly. "But we can change what future our peoples will share." He extended his hands in a gesture of reconciliation.

The Progenitor leader Gorhan stood in response. He appeared moved by Wellshire's grace. "You honor us with your wisdom, Secretary," Gorhan replied. "We will strive to be worthy of your trust."

The mood in the room seemed to shift and lighten. There was hope. Jessica sensed both groups were ready to talk openly and forge a new relationship unburdened by the past.

She caught Vorlus' eye, and his expression softened from remorse to gratitude. Jessica felt confident he would be a steadfast partner going forward. There would still be struggle and uncertainty ahead. But for now, a critical foundation had been laid.

Wellshire smiled warmly. "Then let us begin."

Wellshire and Gorhan sat back down across from each other, the atmosphere now calmer and more hopeful. Jessica felt profoundly moved by the grace and wisdom these leaders had shown in turning a painful revelation into an opportunity for healing.

Secretary Wellshire spoke first. "Tell us, where should we begin in forging a new relationship of mutual understanding between human and Progenitor?"

Gorhan considered the question thoughtfully before responding. "Perhaps it would help our two peoples to interact more regularly beyond just official diplomacy. We have remained too isolated from one another."

Murmurs of agreement came from both groups. Jessica nodded along, thinking of the gulf of mystery that still surrounded the Progenitors to most humans.

Gorhan continued "I propose an exchange program, allowing individuals from both our cultures to immerse themselves in the other." He turned to Wellshire with a look of cautious optimism. "The bonds formed could anchor our new friendship."

Wellshire smiled broadly. "What an inspired suggestion! I can think of no better way for our peoples to learn empathy for one another."

He stood again and extended a hand to Gorhan who rose to grasp it firmly. "Let it be so. The wonders ahead for both our cultures through open exchange are greater than any divisions of the past."

Jessica felt a thrill run through her. She had helped set these extraordinary events in motion simply by following scientific truth wherever it led. What other amazing discoveries lay ahead that could unlock even greater understanding? For the first time, imagining a collaborative future with the Progenitors held more wonder than uncertainty.

As the meeting adjourned, Jessica approached Vorlus who had first opened her mind to this new realm of possibility between their species. "I believe we will do great things together," she said warmly.

Vorlus' eyes crinkled in a smile. "As do I, my friend."

Chapter 6

Jessica took a deep, centering breath as she prepared to embark on the inaugural exchange visit to the Progenitors' central planet. She double checked that her translator implant was securely fastened to her jacket lapel and that her luggage was stowed. This trip represented a historic step toward mutual understanding between their species. As one of the first human exchange envoys, she felt both thrilled and humbled by the opportunity and responsibility.

The transport ship reminded Jessica of a sleek, futuristic bullet train, but capable of traversing light years while passengers were in suspended animation. Vorlus met her at the platform when she boarded.

"Welcome aboard!" he said warmly. "How are you feeling about the journey ahead?"

"Nervous, but excited," Jessica admitted. "I've been imagining this since I was a child looking up at the stars."

Vorlus nodded knowingly. "And now the dream becomes real. The first of many exchanges to come."

He showed Jessica to a seat that contours to fit her physiology. It reminded her that she was still in many ways a stranger here. But if all went well, that would soon change.

The transport glided smoothly into a trans-stellar tunnel. Vorlus took a seat beside Jessica as the cabin lights dimmed, indicating the initiation of suspended animation for the long voyage.

"When you wake, you'll be in our capital city," Vorlus said. "I hope you'll come to see it as a second home." He smiled warmly before closing his eyes.

Jessica took one last look around at the futuristic interior and then let her eyes drift shut, feeling sleep overtake her. When she opened them again, she would be the first human to ever wake up on the Progenitor homeworld. A mix of nerves and excitement for the historic moment welled up as the cryo-sleep took hold.

When Jessica regained consciousness, it was to a scene almost beyond imagination. It took a moment for her groggy mind to recall where she was. Then it hit her—she was on the Progenitor home planet! She sat up quickly, heart racing with excitement and awe at the realization.

Outside the transport's window, an incredible skyline greeted her. Sweeping towers and domed structures in shimmering metals and glass reached for the sky in graceful curves. Sleek vehicles buzzed between them through the air and on multiple levels of roadways crisscrossing the massive city. It was a vista more magnificent than the most imaginative sci-fi vids back home.

"Incredible, isn't it?" Vorlus had entered unnoticed and now smiled at Jessica's obvious wonder. "Welcome to Calaria, our capital and crown jewel."

Jessica tore her eyes away to face him. "It's breathtaking," she said sincerely. "Thank you again for this opportunity."

As they disembarked, a female Progenitor approached them on the platform. She wore a layered robe in vibrant hues of purple and blue.

"Ah, here is Leyliana, one of our foremost archivists," Vorlus introduced her. "She will help orient you to our history and culture while here."

Leyliana folded her hands and bowed graciously. "Well met, Jessica of Earth. We hope you find your time here enlightening." Her voice was melodic and her eyes kind. Jessica instantly liked her.

They took a transport capsule along a sparkling aerial thoroughfare, weaving between soaring towers. Jessica peppered Leyliana with questions, her scientific curiosity overflowing. She learned about the city's ingenious renewable energy system, its masterful vertical design, and integration of nature. Leyliana spoke with obvious pride for her home. As Jessica gazed out the transport capsule's window, she marveled at the alien beauty of the architecture below. The sweeping towers and domes that made up most of the cityscape seemed to defy gravity with their curved, asymmetrical forms.

The structures gleamed in silver, gold, and iridescent colors Jessica couldn't name, with intricate geometric patterns adorning many façades. She glimpsed lush gardens and water features nestled magically between buildings without disrupting the overall harmonious design.

"Your structures are stunning," Jessica remarked to Leyliana. "What are some of the major architectural influences?"

Leyliana's eyes lit up, pleased at Jessica's cultural curiosity. "Early on, the style you see appeared organically from our materials and mathematics. We built upward for efficiency and incorporated nature."

She pointed out a massive dome with a rainbow diffraction pattern. "That is our main scientific academy. The prismatic effect symbolizes how knowledge unifies all fields."

An architectural wonder unfolded next to three towers intertwining like an opened blossom. "Our cultural arts consortium," Leyliana explained. "Each tower represents one of our artistic disciplines."

Jessica was enthralled by the philosophical meaning encoded in the buildings' designs. She eagerly asked question after question as they continued the descent, awed by this fusion of art, nature and technology that was so uniquely Progenitor. She couldn't wait to experience more.

As they descended to ground level, Jessica saw her first Progenitor citizens up close. They gazed at her with what she guessed was curiosity and friendly wariness. She realized she must seem as alien to them as they did to her. The thought gave her an idea how to break the ice.

"May I ask your names?" she inquired of a group gathered in a park-like garden. Their surprise turned to delight at her effort to connect. Soon they were conversing merrily, exchanging introductions and questions back and forth. Jessica's heart swelled. This was just the beginning.

After the first architectural tour, Leyliana brought Jessica to the guest quarters where she would be staying. The rooms were spacious and filled with plush furnishings and interactive artworks that responded to touch. Floor-to-ceiling windows looked out on a tranquil garden and fish pond. It was more luxurious than any hotel Jessica had seen on Earth.

"I hope you find this accommodation comfortable during your stay," Leyliana said politely.

"Are you kidding? This is incredible!" Jessica said, running her hands over the exotic materials of the furnishings. She paused at a shelf displaying a row of ornate metal sculptures. "May I?"

"Of course, they are yours to enjoy," Leyliana replied.

Jessica carefully picked one up, turning it over in her hands. Abstract shapes curled and twisted in asymmetric patterns that resembled plants or sea creatures from an alien ocean. She was struck by the tactile pleasure of following each intricate curve with her fingers.

"The artist is quite renowned," Leyliana commented. "Her name is Ellisan. She takes inspiration from mathematics and nature."

Jessica made a mental note to learn more about Progenitor art styles during her stay. She was intrigued by how their aesthetic tastes and values might reflect their history and worldviews.

Over a lavish meal of colorful cuisine Jessica could not begin to name, Leyliana gave her an overview of the schedule for the next day.

"I thought we would start with a tour of the oldest district," she suggested. "It showcases our ancient architecture." Leyliana handed Jessica what looked like a slender metal wand. "This is for you, to access our networks and databases. It will translate any data you query."

Eagerly, Jessica scrolled through the device, amazed by the amount of knowledge available with a simple flick. "This is incredible, thank you!"

Leyliana smiled. "Full access to our libraries is one of the greatest gifts our leadership feels we can offer your people. Knowledge belongs to all."

Later that evening, Jessica sat by the window watching the city lights glow as her mind swirled with all she had experienced and learned already. She could hardly fall asleep, too excited about the day to come. There was so much yet to discover about this astonishing civilization she was privileged to glimpse.

The next morning Jessica awoke energized and ready to dive back in. Over a delicious meal of sweet golden fruit, Leyliana outlined their day's agenda. Jessica quickly gulped down the last bite of her breakfast fruit and eagerly followed Leyliana outside into the bustling capital. She was ready to fully immerse herself in the Progenitor city.

Leyliana led her down crystalline walkways overflowing with sleek hover vehicles and citizens going about their days. The aromatic scents of food vendors and gardens wafted by as Jessica struggled to take in all the sights and sounds. Everything was new and exciting.

They rode a transport capsule out of the central district to an area with simpler architecture and broader thoroughfares. Leyliana explained this was the oldest part of the city, built soon after the Progenitors' arrival millennia ago. Jessica could see the cruder fabrication techniques that spoke of an earlier era, but it had aged gracefully with character.

Winding side streets revealed open-air marketplaces teeming with merchants selling elaborate textiles, artisanal crafts, fresh produce, and other wares. Jessica picked up items here and there, smiling as she tried to decipher their purpose or artistry. The patient merchants answered her eager questions, showing Progenitor hospitality.

Turning a corner, a sudden hush fell over the market. All activity ceased as citizens stared in Jessica's direction. She realized in this neighborhood, her presence was likely a first. Self-consciously, she gave a small wave and hesitant smile. A few returned the gesture while others simply watched her curiously.

Leyliana placed a reassuring hand on Jessica's shoulder. "Do not worry, they will come to accept you in time. Your visit is a step in the right direction." Heartened, Jessica continued exploring, determined to represent humanity well through openness and respect.

By day's end, her feet were sore, but Jessica felt exhilarated. She returned to her quarters still buzzing from all she had seen. Her data wand flickered with a message from Secretary-General Wellshire; Earth awaited her dispatch eagerly. Smiling, Jessica began recording her impressions to share. It was just her first day, but already she had so much to tell.

The next day, Leyliana escorted Jessica to the renowned Sky Gardens, a series of lush rooftop parks and conservatories towering above the city. As they strolled along winding pathways through exotic flora from across the Progenitor worlds, Jessica felt her stress and fatigue melt away.

The warmth of the third sun filtering through the greenery gave the gardens an otherworldly glow. Musicians played haunting melodies on stringed instruments while patrons dined at outdoor cafes. Jessica was entranced by the oasis of beauty and tranquility amidst the bustling metropolis.

Afterward, they visited the hydraulic power complex which converted tidal energies from the planet's oceans into electricity. Jessica admired the simple elegance of the design and took holos to send back to her colleagues on Earth. She hoped such creative engineering solutions might inspire human cities as well.

At a lively educational center, young Progenitor children observed Jessica with more curiosity than fear. Their innocent, genuine questions made her laugh and reminded her of students back home. Jessica felt hope that the next generation held promise for even greater interspecies connection.

Throughout the day's explorations, most citizens regarded Jessica with cautious interest, though some still hung back uneasily. In the market, gleaming jewels carved from shells caught her eye. She admired the crystalline star charts and handwoven blankets as well. Each unique handicraft reflected this planet's beauty and artistry.

By evening, Jessica's feet ached pleasantly from walking countless miles. Her data wand overflowed with notes, holos and discoveries to share. Though still an outsider here in many ways, she was slowly feeling more at home. She couldn't wait to see what hidden marvels the next day's explorations might uncover across this fascinating alien society.

The next several days passed in a whirlwind of sights and activities as Leyliana guided Jessica all over the capital. She visited the renowned orbital laboratories where Progenitor scientists studied anomalies in deep space. At a theater, she was enthralled by a stunning aerial acrobatic performance that seemed to defy gravity.

Every day her integration into Progenitor society deepened. The wary curiosity she was met with at first gradually warmed into friendly greetings and conversations. The language implant allowed her to pick up the intricate native tongue quickly.

Soon she was bargaining enthusiastically with vendors in markets, chatting with locals over meals at cozy cafes, and exchanging ideas with students and academics. She became a minor celebrity; citizens would request holos with her to share the historic encounter.

Jessica was sad when it came time for Leyliana to leave for other duties. But Vorlus assured her the work of connection would continue.

"Leyliana set you on the path, now you must walk it yourself," he advised. "But know that my door is always open, my friend."

On her own, Jessica felt both liberated and intimidated. But she had come too far to balk at the challenge. That day she set off into the city, determined to forge bonds not as a human ambassador, but as Jessica—explorer, scientist, and now honorary Progenitor.

She soon found herself discussing astronomy with a noted university scholar, marveling at rare off-planet specimens in the natural history museum and being soundly defeated at chess by a grinning Progenitor child in the park.

Tired but fulfilled, Jessica returned to her quarters with a warm sense of belonging growing within her. In such a short time, this advanced civilization felt more like a second home than she had dreamed possible. She wondered if the Progenitors back on Earth were having a similar experience of interconnection. She hoped Secretary Wellshire could see the promise in what they had started here.

Chapter 7

Secretary-General Gabriel Wellshire gazed out the window of his New York office, lost in thought. Far below, ant-like hovers buzzed between glittering towers in the evening light. But Wellshire's mind was light years away, pondering the implications of Jessica's dispatches from the Progenitor homeworld.

Her reports brimmed with enthusiastic discoveries: alien architecture and artworks, innovative sustainable technologies, glimpses into their rich cultural and intellectual life. But most promising was the gradual dissolving of barriers as she formed connections at the personal level.

Wellshire hoped similar seeds of understanding were taking root on Earth. The Progenitor exchange envoys sent here were dispersed in cities worldwide. Feedback thus far has been positive if cautious. There had been minor incidents: suspicious looks, turned backs, whispers. But also, breakthroughs—shy conversations slowly warming, hands outstretched in greeting.

He knew this emotional journey would not be rushed. But Jessica's vivid insights gave him faith in their species' shared ability to open their minds and hearts when shown the way.

Not through politics or grand gestures, but the patient work of building relationships.

A knock interrupted Wellshire's contemplation. His senior aide Alice Evans entered, tablet in hand.

"Sorry to disturb you, Mr. Secretary, but we just received an urgent message flagged highest priority."

Wellshire frowned. "What is it, Alice?"

"It's the Progenitor envoy in Los Angeles, sir. He was assaulted leaving his hotel this morning. Beaten badly before security intervened." Alice's face was grim.

Wellshire's heart sank. He should have expected the hatred of a few outweighing the goodwill of many. "How is he?"

"Recovering but shaken. His team has requested he return home at once for security reasons."

"I see." Wellshire sighed deeply, saddened but unsurprised by this dark turn. "Let us not judge all humanity by its worst actors. Fear breeds fear. Our response must be compassion."

Alice nodded firmly. "I agree, sir."

Wellshire joined her in front of the window overlooking New York City, this microcosm of human diversity and potential. Somewhere out there, the seeds Jessica planted were starting to take root. But they would need tending through the storms ahead.

"Please have my office draft a personal apology to their delegation. We must remind them of the promise we saw, remind ourselves," Wellshire said. Alice smiled proudly at his wise grace.

Wellshire gazed out at the city lights flickering to life as a new night fell. But darkness did not last forever. He had seen humanity's light pierce it before. This was but the first test.

More would come, but hope lived on in people's hearts. He clasped his hands, contemplating their next steps.

Wellshire sat down with Alice to discuss how to thoughtfully respond to this act of violence against their Progenitor guest. They needed to balance accountability and compassion.

"Has the attacker been identified and taken into custody?" Wellshire asked.

Alice nodded. "Yes, it was a lone assailant—a radical xenophobe unfortunately swayed by dangerous anti-alien conspiracy rhetoric." She shook her head in dismay.

"A product of fear and ignorance," Wellshire said sadly. "We must pursue justice but also prevent further hate from spreading." An idea struck him. "Perhaps this tragedy can become an opportunity to strengthen the bonds between our species."

Alice looked intrigued. "What do you propose, sir?"

"A gathering of human and Progenitor leaders from around Earth to publicly condemn this attack. We reaffirm our commitment to interspecies community and peace."

Alice smiled. "A wonderful thought, Mr. Secretary. That kind of solidarity is exactly what's needed now."

She shifted her tone. "However, we just received another urgent update. Chicago's Progenitor envoy has requested to cut her visit short and return home. She reports feeling increasingly unsafe and unwelcome by many citizens there."

Wellshire sighed deeply, his earlier optimism deflating. "I feared more such reactions. We are asking much of them."

"There is still hope, sir," Alice encouraged. "Several other envoys replied, urging patience and understanding. The roots are there, if we keep nurturing them."

Wellshire smiled gratefully at her faith when his own wavered. "You're absolutely right, Alice. We'll move forward with our plans."

He stood with renewed vigor. "Please arrange that gathering. In times of tension, we must come together. Our friends need solidarity, humanity's better angels reminding them of our shared hopes."

Alice nodded firmly and turned to make the calls, buoyed by Wellshire's determination. Watching her, Wellshire felt his hope reignite. There would be setbacks and struggles ahead. But people like Alice assured him this dream would live on.

The gathering took shape over the next few days as Secretary Wellshire's office coordinated with community leaders. A diverse coalition committed to attending: politicians, activists, artists and religious figures. Progenitor representatives still remaining on Earth also agreed to join and share their experiences.

Wellshire gazed out at the crowd assembling in New York's central park on the sunny morning of the event. A temporary stage stood surrounded by thousands of humans and Progenitors intermingled, awaiting his address. Media drones hovered nearby to broadcast his words worldwide.

Stepping to the podium, Wellshire looked out at the expectant faces. He spotted the young Progenitor student who had been attacked, still bearing the wounds, but standing proudly. Wellshire's heart swelled with emotion.

"My friends," he began somberly. "Negativity can't drive out the negative. Only positivity can do that." Murmurs of assent rippled through the crowd.

"The violence inflicted recently on our esteemed guests shadows our shared hopes. But today we rekindle the light of peace, understanding and justice." Thunderous applause erupted. The Progenitor student nodded graciously at Wellshire's words.

Wellshire's voice rang out firmly over the crowd. "Let all peoples see your spirit here today. As we link arms in unity, ignorance and fear flee before our solidarity."

The passionate cheers grew louder, humans and Progenitors alike raising their voices together. Wellshire stepped back, overwhelmed by the love and promise shining on all their faces as one. This dream would not be extinguished. Their enthusiasm would guide the way forward.

As the crowd dispersed in hopeful spirits, Wellshire approached the Progenitor student who had been attacked. "Your courage inspires me beyond words," Wellshire said, taking the young Progenitor's hands in heartfelt thanks.

"As you have inspired mine," he replied warmly. "Do not lose faith in the goodness within your people. One day we will all live as one."

Wellshire smiled gratefully. "Of that I have no doubt. Together is how we will heal and rise." The young Progenitor smiled back, seeing the future emerging from positivity.

Following the gathering, Secretary Wellshire diligently pursued avenues of healing and justice. The attacker was sentenced to rehabilitation therapy rather than prison. Wellshire arranged for him to meet the Progenitor he had assaulted and learn about his life and humanity. A documentary crew filmed their emotional journey from hatred to forgiveness.

When aired globally, the documentary became a touchstone for communities worldwide grappling with the changes happening around them. Its raw depiction of reconciliation resonated across divides. Forgiveness and openness were contagious.

Wellshire also launched a series of youth exchange programs, connecting classrooms in different cities and the Progenitor planet. Children gazed with wonder at their counterparts light years away. Their innocent curiosity sowed seeds of interspecies friendship that would blossom into a more harmonious future.

Jessica's dispatches from the Progenitor homeworld continued flowing to Wellshire's office, each more enthusiastic than the last. She described the planet's richly unique ecosystems she was able to experience during an expedition to the remotest wilderness. She marveled at the symbiosis between nature and technology that allowed such environments to thrive in balance.

Most promising was the warm camaraderie blossoming between Jessica and the researchers she accompanied. At night around campfires under unfamiliar constellations, they found common ground in their shared spirit of exploration.

Wellshire drew hope from Jessica's tales, knowing she represented Earth's highest ideals as an ambassador of humanity's potential. He only wished he could share her experiences firsthand. An idea sparked.

Why don't I visit the Progenitor planet myself? Wellshire mused. An unprecedented journey could catalyze even greater interspecies connection.

Soon, he stood before a stunned press conference sharing his plans for the first diplomatic mission by a human Secretary to the Progenitor homeworld. Questions flooded in, but Wellshire silenced the clamor with a raised hand.

"We have turned the first pages in a new chapter of mankind's history, but many chapters remain unwritten," he said. "We must keep advancing together. My friends, I embark on this journey not for its risks, but for its promise. Please, wish me godspeed."

Wellshire's pulse raced with anticipation and purpose as the sleek prototype transport capsule made final preparations for launch. The entire planet's eyes were upon this trailblazing mission of peace. He was ready to take those first steps into a larger galaxy, forging bonds between worlds.

Strapped into the pilot's seat, Wellshire watched streaming stars morph into dazzling tunnels of light outside the cockpit windows as the ship's hyperdrives engaged. In mere hours he would reach his destination and embrace Jessica, a shining beacon of all they had dreamed.

But when the transport capsule dropped out of hyperdrive, Wellshire quickly realized something was wrong. An ominous field of debris greeted him instead of the crystalline Progenitor homeworld he had seen in holos.

"Jessica...what has happened here?" Wellshire gasped. Emergency proximity alarms suddenly blared a warning as the battered remains of unfamiliar alien warships appeared from the rubble, weapons trained on his defenseless vessel.

Wellshire sat stunned as the imposing alien warships surrounded his tiny vessel. How could a peaceful planet have become this ominous graveyard so suddenly?

Before he could react, a tractor beam seized the transport capsule, drawing it into the hangar bay of the largest warship. Helpless, Wellshire could only watch as armored soldiers approached to cut open the cockpit. Rough claws yanked him from his seat and down the ramp.

Wellshire raised his hands in surrender. "I mean no harm! I am Secretary Wellshire of Earth seeking the Progenitor homeworld," he explained calmly. The imposing soldiers said nothing, marching him down the cold gray corridors into the depths of the massive ship.

Wellshire was brought before a towering creature draped in black, exuding menace. "My name is Secretary Wellshire of–"

"I know who you are, human," the figure boomed. "You are a fool to come here. This system now belongs to the Zijkhal Empire."

Wellshire's mind raced, but he kept an even tone. "Please, I was invited by the Progenitors as an ambassador. If there is a conflict, let us discuss a diplomatic resolution."

The Zijkhal commander laughed coldly. "Ignorant creature. There is nothing left of the weak Progenitors. Our armada crushed their defenses in days and bombarded their world into oblivion."

Wellshire reeled in horror. How could Jessica's wondrous second home have been utterly destroyed? Rage and despair battled within him, but he calmed himself. He had to be tactful to survive.

"Destroying is easy. Building community and trust across differences is hard," Wellshire said carefully. "I understand you value strength, but true strength lies in wisdom and restraint."

The Zijkhal commander sneered. "Enough naïve chatter. You have two choices—join our empire's expansion or be annihilated." He waved his clawed hand and soldiers seized Wellshire.

Thinking fast, Wellshire spoke up. "Wait! Journeying here took immense resources and innovative technology beyond your current capabilities. Earth can offer knowledge and skills to bolster your empire peacefully."

The Zijkhal commander paused, considering. Wellshire pressed his luck. "Or if you prefer force, you may find conquering my planet more difficult than you imagine. We have defenses and allies across the galaxy." Wellshire hoped his bluff sounded convincing.

Silently the Zijkhal commander weighed Wellshire's words. Finally, he waved his soldiers off. "Very well, we will bring you back to our central planet for now." He leaned in close to Wellshire's face, baring sharp teeth. "But any deception will be punished by immediate death."

The journey to the Zijkhal commander's home world gave Wellshire time to think over his predicament. He grieved the Progenitors, hoping some had escaped. But he had to focus on saving Earth. Perhaps he could find a faction of Zijkhal more receptive to his appeals.

Upon landing, Wellshire was ushered into a dazzling citadel of obsidian towers. The Zijkhal commander ordered lavish quarters prepared for their unusual guest. Wellshire was guarded closely but treated well, still too intriguing to eliminate outright.

However, the Zijkhal commander avoided his persistent efforts at dialogue. Frustrated, Wellshire decided to change tack. Slipping away from his distracted guards, he stealthily explored the citadel's labyrinthine corridors, eavesdropping for hints about Zijkhal culture. The ornate shrines and sculptures suggested a deeply spiritual people beneath their harsh exterior.

Finally, Wellshire slipped unnoticed into a massive courtyard where thousands of Zijkhal prostrated before a towering pyramidal altar in silent prayer. Among their chanting rose gasps as they noticed Wellshire's presence. He raised his hands in cautious respect, then slowly knelt and bowed his head, miming their rituals.

A murmur rippled through the crowd. Breaking protocol, some approached this outsider, curious and unafraid. "You honor our ways," an elder said, impressed. Wellshire smiled and nodded, sensing an opportunity in their wonder. Perhaps peace still had a chance here.

Chapter 8

Staring up at the massive pyramid altar, Secretary Wellshire knew this was his chance to connect with the spiritual heart of the Zijkhal. As they chanted and swayed, he allowed his mind to open to their rhythmic rituals, letting his guards down. To his surprise, he found a sense of transcendent calm and unity flowing into him.

The elder Zijkhal who had spoken to him extended a clawed hand. "Come, share in our sacraments." Warily, Wellshire accepted and followed him through a towering archway guarded by armored warriors, leaving the rest of the praying Zijkhal behind.

They descended through dim torch-lit passages depicting ancient Zijkhal battles in intricate carvings along the walls. Wellshire wanted to stop and study them for clues about his captor's past but had to quicken his pace to match the sweeping strides of his guide.

At last, they emerged into a cavernous chamber lined with more ceremonial pyramids. A gathering of imposing Zijkhal garbed in black awaited them solemnly. At the far end stood a massive snakclike statue with hundreds of carved eyes staring, clasping a blazing sphere in its coils. Heat washed over Wellshire as they approached the odd shrine.

The elder knelt before the strange monument, chanting in reverent tones. Wellshire carefully copied his posture and closed his eyes, trying to tap back into the meditative state he had felt earlier. To his surprise, it returned stronger than before. The flames seemed to pierce through his shut eyelids, opening a vision in his mind.

He saw twin bronze moons shining over a red desert landscape. Multitudes of lizard-like bipeds in primitive clothing sat around sacred fires, faces upturned to the moons in worship. Somehow Wellshire basically understood—this was a glimpse into the foundational era of Zijkhal civilization millennia ago.

The vision shifted, now showing Zijkhal clad for war. They wielded cruel axes, conquering nearby tribes. As they dominated more worlds, their culture shifted from spiritual tradition to military might. The flames in the statue's eyes slowly dwindled as each world fell before Zijkhal supremacy.

Wellshire was startled from his trance as the elder finished the incantation. The gathered Zijkhal were staring at Wellshire curiously. Had they sensed what he saw? Carefully avoiding their gaze, he bowed his head respectfully again. The elder spoke.

"You are the first outsider to see these sacred icons and share in our most ancient rites." His tone held intrigue rather than anger at Wellshire's audacious infiltration.

Wellshire chose his next words carefully. "I am honored to glimpse the rich heritage of your people beyond the might I have seen. In our diversity lies potential for mutual understanding."

The elder scowled, past optimism fading. "Bold words after you trespassed uninvited in deception. Our worlds are better apart." He gestured for guards to take Wellshire away.

"Wait, please," Wellshire begged. "I mean no ill will. Violence will only breed more violence endlessly. There are other paths, if we have the courage to walk them together."

The elder paused. For a moment Wellshire sensed his words had struck a chord. But the guards gripped Wellshire's arms, their leader's expression growing colder. "Your naive idealism is not welcome here. Be grateful we let you live at all."

As he was dragged back through the torch-lit corridors, Wellshire's hopes sank. But he knew in his vision lay the key to reaching these beings. If their spiritual past could be reawakened, their culture might change course. But how?

The Zijkhal guards marched Secretary Wellshire back through the citadel's maze of obsidian corridors until they reached his lavish quarters. They roughly shoved him inside and sealed the doors behind him.

Wellshire paced the chamber, replaying the strange visions from the shrine in his mind. He was so close to setting up a genuine connection. If he could just reconnect the Zijkhal's current rulers with their own forgotten spiritual roots, he was convinced their aggression could transform into openness.

But bridging that gap would not be easy. He would need an ally within Zijkhal society privy to the past who could guide him. Wellshire slumped down on the extravagant bed, trying to formulate a plan.

A faint sound came from the wall—a scraping of stone. Wellshire sat up, listening closely. A section of carved obsidian panels suddenly shifted, and a hidden passage opened. A lone

Zijkhal slipped into Wellshire's room, clad in a simple robe rather than armor.

Wellshire stood cautiously as the Zijkhal approached. "Be calm, friend. I am no enemy," he said in a hushed tone. "Word spread of the outsider who breached the sacred shrine. You wish to know our true past?"

Wellshire studied the Zijkhal's weathered, honest features and decided to take a chance. "Yes, I seek to understand your people beyond the surface. Violence breeds more violence. Another way must be possible."

The Zijkhal nodded solemnly. "Yes, those of us who remember the old ways know the truth lies in our ancient spiritual roots, not conquest and might."

He continued, "My name is Zajid. I guard the songs and stories of our forebears when moon time rites illuminated our path."

Zajid drew closer to Wellshire. "Close your eyes. I will sing the melodies that open the heart and spirit." Wellshire sat and closed his eyes. Zajid began a low rhythmic chant in an ancient tongue.

Wellshire's mind was transported back to the red deserts from his vision. But now he could see the details vividly. Gentle bronze-scaled Zijkhal sitting around fires, younglings dreaming under the stars. The twin moons' light guided hunters and nourished crops. Life followed lunar cycles and seasons in harmony.

Zajid's songs shifted to tones of grief and warning. Flames turned to black smoke as Zijkhal armies conquered all in their path, forsaking spirit for might. The same statue Wellshire had seen earlier wept molten tears as darkness fell over culture and soul.

The melodies softened to hope as Wellshire opened his eyes. Zajid smiled kindly, seeing the songs had awakened true understanding in this visitor.

"Thank you, my friend," Wellshire said. "But how can we remind your people of who they once were? Their salvation lies in rediscovering their spiritual past."

Zajid's smile faded. "The conquerors cling to power. They believe spirit makes one weak and to be feared." He sighed heavily. "I do not know if they can be swayed."

Wellshire grasped Zajid's clawed hands firmly. "There is always hope if the will is strong enough. Your songs opened my eyes, and they can open your elders' hearts too."

Zajid thought carefully, then nodded. "Perhaps if outsiders remind us of our lost way, we may change these truths to become real again even for rulers." He pointed to the sky. "The time of special moons is soon. Join us in the rites that may sway them."

Wellshire felt a spark of hope ignite within him. "I will do whatever it takes."

Zajid quickly showed Wellshire the hidden passage. "This way you can slip down to the shrines unseen. I will guide you in the old rites when you arrive." He placed a gnarled hand on Wellshire's shoulder. "Our redemption lies with you now, friend. Be wise and strong."

As Zajid slipped away, Wellshire steeled himself for the monumental trial ahead. An entire civilization's fate rested on reviving its own forgotten light before evil consumed it entirely. He had to try, for their sake and Earth's. Stepping into the passage, he descended toward destiny.

Wellshire made his way down the hidden passage, guided only by faint torchlight reflecting off the ornate obsidian walls. The path sloped steadily downward, taking him deep below the Zijkhal citadel. He wondered how close he was getting to the sacred shrines.

After what felt like hours, he reached the end of the passage. Extinguishing his torch, Wellshire squeezed through a narrow opening into one of the massive cavernous shrines. It appeared empty for now, lit only by the reddish glow of the snake statue's flaming orb.

Keeping to the shadows, Wellshire crept along the shrine's perimeter towards the archway leading to the central worship chamber. He froze as a patrol of Zijkhal guards strode through, oblivious to his presence.

Once they passed, Wellshire slipped through the towering arch into the massive courtyard where he had first mingled unnoticed with the worshiping crowds. It too now stood eerily empty and silent. The moon rites must take place only at special times.

Wellshire's heart pounded as he scanned for any sign of Zajid. A sound echoed from a far passage—the shuffle of clawed feet. Wellshire darted behind a carved pillar, peering out cautiously as robed figures entered the courtyard in procession.

Among them, Wellshire spotted Zajid carrying an ancient book. They took places circling the central pyramid altar, kneeling in unison. Wellshire hesitated, unsure whether to reveal himself.

Zajid raised his eyes, noticing Wellshire's hidden form. With the slightest nod, he beckoned Wellshire forth. Taking a deep breath, Wellshire stepped out from the shadows and joined the circle. Gasps arose from the other Zijkhal, but Zajid raised a clawed hand, assuring them it was allowed.

As Zajid opened the book, Wellshire saw it was filled with intricate symbols and charts aligned to the phases of the twin moons. Following Zajid's lead, the Zijkhal began chanting, swaying, and tracing complex patterns in the air with their claws by moonlight.

Wellshire did his best to mimic their hypnotic movements and chants. He could feel his limited understanding of their language steadily improving, intuiting meanings more clearly. Their tones spoke of guidance, wisdom, and rebirth.

Gradually, Wellshire noticed shapes moving in the darkness of the chamber's farthest recesses. More Zijkhal were appearing silently from hidden passages, including elders in formal black robes. They looked on with what appeared to be curiosity, making no move to interrupt the rituals.

The new arrivals joined hands, forming an outer ring around the shrine. Their deep resonant voices added new layers to the chanting that raised the hair on the back of Wellshire's neck. He glimpsed Zajid looking hopeful. The lost songs were coming alive again.

Wellshire was unsure how long the entrancing rituals continued. But gradually, he noticed the sky through skylights in the shrine's vaulted ceiling begin to glow. The twin bronze moons, one crescent and one full, rose into view overhead, perfectly aligned.

The Zijkhal rituals reached a crescendo as the moonlight filtered down on them. Wellshire's senses felt electrified by an otherworldly energy in the chamber. He saw tears glistening in many Zijkhal eyes around him. Tonight, their species' soul was reawakening.

But was it enough to convince their leaders to turn from conquest back to spiritual tradition? Wellshire knew the coming hours would decide if pacifism or bloodshed lay in their future. As the moons crossed the sky, he prayed silently to their guiding light.

As the entrancing moonlight rituals finally wound down, Wellshire stood silently among the robed Zijkhal, unsure what would happen next. He was keenly aware of the imposing elders still studying him curiously from the chamber's periphery.

Zajid approached Wellshire, claws clasped warmly. "Thank you, friend. Your presence and open spirit this night brought life back to our ways." He glanced cautiously at the watching elders. "But they will decide if tradition truly returns."

One elder stepped forward, his black robes flowing. The other Zijkhal made way with deep bows as he approached the altar where Wellshire and Zajid stood.

"You defied protocol by invading our most sacred rites," the elder said sternly to Wellshire. "Yet I sense no ill intent in you. Explain yourself, outsider."

Wellshire spoke carefully. "I only wish to understand your people beyond the violence I've seen...to remind you of hope within, not fear without."

Murmurs rose from the surrounding Zijkhal. The elder raised a clawed hand for silence. "Bold claims. Our warriors warned you are a naive fool." His expression was unreadable.

Zajid stepped forward pleadingly. "Yet this stranger heard the songs in his spirit as we have. He knows our peace-woven past concealed even from most Zijkhal now."

The elder processed this. "If true, that is deeply meaningful." He looked Wellshire over critically. "We shall see if your heart is true in the coming days. For now, none may know of these secret rites."

The Zijkhal dispersed back into the hidden passages. Zajid gripped Wellshire's shoulder tightly. "Have hope. The seeds are planted." He then slipped away after the others.

Alone, Wellshire sat at the altar reflecting as the moonlight faded. Had he changed their thinking at all? There was no way to tell yet if the elders would seriously rethink their violent ways. But he had to keep trying.

Footsteps approached in the darkness—more guards come to retrieve their rogue guest. As they escorted Wellshire roughly back through the citadel, he saw new light dawning through skylights. The future remained unwritten for now.

Over the next weeks, Wellshire noticed subtle hints of change amid the strict routines. Whispered conversations fell silent when he entered rooms. Documents vanished quickly when he passed officials in halls.

The Zijkhal remained carefully neutral toward him in public, not revealing whether his daring infiltration had borne fruit. Wellshire grew anxious but kept faith. This was a culture transformed over millennia - patience was essential.

One day, Zajid secretly approached Wellshire in his chambers again via the hidden passage. "Come quickly, friend," he urged. "The elders request your presence."

Heart racing, Wellshire followed Zajid's lead through a dizzying maze of back corridors and stairwells to an extravagant chamber. The black-robed elders sat waiting around a flickering brazier. They motioned for Wellshire to join them.

The head elder spoke solemnly. "We have discussed your unprecedented presence here extensively. Your risky gambit in the shrine shall remain an open secret."

Wellshire chose his next words carefully. "I meant no harm, only hope of finding common ground."

The elder nodded. "Just so...and our meditations since suggest your words have wisdom." He leaned closer to Wellshire, firelight playing across his skeletal features.

"The songs and rites of old stir us from within, yet we rule an empire of might. A difficult balance lies ahead." His tone became grave. "Can conquering spirits again cultivate stillness, acceptance, harmony?

Wellshire replied earnestly, "If your past is a living memory, not mere ruins, faith can lift you to that higher place again."

The elders sat in solemn contemplation. Finally, the head elder spoke again. "You have given us much to ponder deeply. We shall see where this new path leads, if our people can walk it with open souls once more."

They dismissed Wellshire and Zajid with gracious bows. Zajid appeared pleased as they made their way back. "You plant seeds well, my friend. Continue nourishing them and change will grow."

Wellshire nodded, newfound hope rising within him. Maybe peace had a chance here after all.

Chapter 9

Following the moon time rituals, Wellshire noticed a subtle shift in the Zijkhal's demeanor towards him. While still highly formal, their interactions seemed less cold, almost curious. Zajid's encouragement gave him hope, something had clicked in their consciousness.

However, true change comes slowly to ancient civilizations. As Wellshire strolled through the citadel's obsidian corridors one day, he spotted two Zijkhal officials whispering furtively. They halted as he approached, waiting for him to pass before resuming their hushed conference.

Wellshire contemplated the odd encounter as he continued on. Were they merely gossiping about his presence? Or was a contingent emerging that resisted the cultural reawakening he stood for? He resolved to tread cautiously in the days ahead.

Upon returning to his quarters, Wellshire was surprised to find a Zijkhal waiting inside. It was one of the armored warriors that had captured him originally. Wellshire tensed warily.

"What brings you here, friend?" Wellshire asked in a measured tone. The Zijkhal warrior maintained a stony silence, studying Wellshire closely as if trying to interpret his very nature.

After a tense moment, he spoke. "I am Jaaxus, commander of the Black Talon legion." His voice held no overt hostility, simply sizing Wellshire up. "Walk with me, outsider."

Having little choice, Wellshire followed Jaaxus out into the citadel's cavernous halls. Zijkhal they passed stared in surprise but kept their distance. Jaaxus led the way to a secluded parapet looking out on the vast sprawling metropolis surrounding the citadel.

"You have greatly interested the elders, it seems" Jaaxus remarked, gazing out at the alien skyline. "But some of us question whether our people should be so...malleable." He turned to face Wellshire.

Wellshire maintained steady eye contact. "Progress takes courage. But there are always those content with how things are." He kept his tone non-accusatory.

Jaaxus narrowed his serpentine eyes, claws tightening on the parapet's edge. "And often change brings ruin, despite naive hopes." His meaning was clear; Wellshire was meddling in things beyond his grasp.

"Perhaps only the humble truly understand change's cost," Wellshire ventured carefully. "Those who dominate, fear losing most."

He sensed Jaaxus' pride bristling at the implied criticism. Wellshire prepared himself in case the warrior's volatile temper emerged. But Jaaxus merely snorted derisively after a moment's thought.

"Believe what you will. I simply ensure the Zijkhal remain strong, as is my charge." He stared hard at Wellshire, then left without another word.

Wellshire watched Jaaxus recede down the corridor, troubled. Something in the warrior's piercing tones warned that powerful conservative forces would resist a pacifist shift here to the bitter end. Wellshire sighed anxiously. Social change was never smooth.

After the tense encounter, Wellshire noticed troops of Zijkhal soldiers prominently patrolling the citadel halls more often. Their movements seemed orchestrated to intimidate, staring suspiciously at Wellshire when their paths crossed.

Zajid confirmed Wellshire's suspicions when they next met covertly. "Jaaxus and his ilk press the elders daily to expel you. Your ideas anger them." Zajid's expression was grave. "I fear tensions escalate toward crisis."

Wellshire furrowed his brow. "Then we must redouble efforts for open dialogue and goodwill. Extremism grows best in darkness." Zajid nodded solemnly in agreement.

Their planning was interrupted by the approach of multiple Zijkhal guards. Zajid discreetly slipped away down a hidden passage. The lead guard addressed Wellshire bluntly.

"Come with us. Disruption requires investigation." The guards firmly escorted Wellshire deeper into the citadel, neutralizing any attempts at conversation.

Wellshire suppressed a rising sense of dread. Where was this leading? Had reactionary forces finally persuaded the elders to turn on him? Or did chance still remain to sway them toward wisdom?

The guards ushered Wellshire into the towering chamber where he had first stood trial before the imposing council of elders after his arrival. He steeled himself as the guards took positions along the stone walls, leaving him alone before the elders' stern gazes.

The head elder's gravelly voice echoed in the vast chamber. "Grave accusations have been made against you. Explain your actions these past weeks and be warned: falsehood brings only ruin."

Wellshire chose his next words with utmost care. He bowed respectfully before addressing the expectant council of elders. "I have acted only with the hope of nurturing the spiritual seeds within your people. Violence breeds more violence endlessly. There must be another way."

The elders murmured amongst themselves before the head elder responded. "Some argue you poison our society, eroding the strength and will that built our empire." His tone was measured but firm.

"We protected and guided the Zijkhal for eons. Outsiders can't comprehend what darkness we keep at bay. It is no simple choice we now face."

Wellshire nodded solemnly. "I understand your burden all too well. But light shines brightest against shadow." He met the elder's timeworn gaze. "Has my presence brought anything but illumination gently shared?"

More heated whispers filled the chamber. Wellshire perceived the council was divided, some still clinging to old fears, others seeing wisdom in change. The head elder raised a clawed hand for order before addressing Wellshire again.

"Your intentions seem just, and we do not doubt your spirit's sincerity." He paused, as if carefully considering each word. "But some actions can set events in motion that none can steer."

His eyes bored into Wellshire's. "Tread with wisdom and care in all things. The consequences may be far greater than you know."

With that cryptic warning, the guards escorted Wellshire from the chamber, leaving him to ponder the elder's meaning. Had revealing their cultural past set them on an irreversible course now? He wished desperately to discuss the trial with Zajid but saw no sign of his friend.

Over the next several days, an ominous tension pervaded the citadel's obsidian halls. Patrols of guards eyed Wellshire suspiciously, while officials seemed to slip into shadowy corners whispering as he passed. Jaaxus and his warriors were nowhere to be seen.

Wellshire grew more anxious with each day, jumping at faint sounds. He longed to speak with Zajid and gain insight on the brewing unrest, but his guide seemed to have vanished. Dark premonitions filled Wellshire's thoughts.

Late one sleepless night, Wellshire heard scraping behind the ornamental wall panels of his quarters. He sat up hopefully as a concealed passage opened. But rather than Zajid, three unfamiliar Zijkhal stepped out, clad in black garb.

Wellshire stood cautiously as they approached him silently. Their leader wore a pendant etched with a strange jagged symbol. His cold slit-pupil eyes stared intensely at Wellshire.

"You spread like a sickness in our midst, weakening what was strong," he hissed. "We of the True Talon shall excise you." They moved to surround Wellshire menacingly.

Wellshire raised his hands peaceably. "Friends, let us speak together first before rash action. There need be no strife between us." But their claws unsheathed as they closed in.

Suddenly, the door to Wellshire's quarters burst open. Zajid stormed in, followed by citadel guards. "Back, heretics!" Zajid cried. The intruders turned with angry snarls but hesitated at the sight of the guards.

"Seize them!" Zajid ordered. The guards rushed forward. After a brief clash, two of the attackers were subdued, though the leader managed to disappear back down the hidden passageway.

Zajid grasped Wellshire's shoulder firmly with relief. "Are you harmed, my friend?" Wellshire shook his head, still shaken. Zajid's expression was grave.

"The True Talon faction festers like a canker if unchecked. But perhaps now the elders truly see the threat." He glanced with disdain at their two captured attackers.

Wellshire faced them. "Who are you? Why do this?" One assailant glared back silently, but the other wore a defiant grin. "We are the fangs that guard the jugular while the naive sleep." He spat at Wellshire's feet.

Zajid backhanded the insolent fanatic. "Enough! You are not warriors, merely savage beasts." He ordered them taken away by the guards.

As passions cooled, Zajid turned to Wellshire with an earnest look. "Stay strong, friend. With light, this darkness shall pass." Reassured, Wellshire grasped Zajid's clawed hand. Their road remained long, but hope persisted.

After the attack, Zajid insisted Wellshire be moved to more secure quarters deep within the elders' own sanctum. Patrols were doubled outside his door, yet Wellshire struggled to find calm. He kept reliving the cold fanaticism in the eyes of his assailants.

Zajid did his best to reassure Wellshire when they next met. "The elders have banished the worst extremists from the capital. In time their hatred will fade." Yet Wellshire sensed Zajid was also unsettled by the violent confrontation.

They had known change here would not come easily, but malicious forces seemed determined to prevent reconciliation at any cost. Darkness most fiercely fights the dawn, Zajid observed philosophically. Wellshire took some small comfort in his friend's wisdom.

After several tense weeks without incident, some of Wellshire's anxiety eased. Perhaps reason truly was prevailing within Zijikhal society. The guards' vigilance relaxed slightly in the peaceful sanctuary of the inner citadel.

Late one evening, Wellshire sat reading Zijikhal historical texts Zajid had gifted him, struggling through the intricate scripts. A barely audible click from the door lock startled him. Wellshire froze, listening intently. Had he imagined it?

Suddenly the door burst open and a black garbed Zijikhal charged in wielding a serrated blade. Wellshire dove behind a stone pedestal as the assassin lunged. Shouts rang out in the hall. Seconds later Zajid rushed in with guards.

"Halt, villain!" Zajid cried, grabbing the attacker. The assassin twisted violently, slicing Zajid's arm before the guards could wrestle him down. Zajid grimaced, clutching the wound.

Wellshire rushed over. "Are you badly injured, my friend?" Zajid shook his head. "Just a scratch–I am only glad you are unharmed." He stared gravely down at the hissing fanatic.

The failed attack sent shockwaves through the citadel. Wellshire had come within a hair's breadth of death at the hands of the True Talon yet again. Zajid insisted on personally overseeing security for his friend.

Several days later, Zajid arrived to urgently usher Wellshire through hidden passages up to the highest peak of the central pyramid. "The council eagerly awaits you, my friend. This horror spurs them to decisive action at last."

Wellshire emerged into the blinding sunlight of an open-air platform atop the massive pyramid. The council of elders sat waiting, grim expressions on their skeletal faces. Zajid bowed and stepped aside.

The head elder spoke gravely. "Once again, these heretics of the so-called True Talon strike from the darkness at the heart of our society." His claws scraped the stone seat.

"But no more! By the blood they spilled all Zijkhal extremists who oppose reconciliation with the Progenitors, we hereby name them Khurzan–the Forsaken–and banish all their ilk from our cities." His proclamation echoed across the capital.

The other elders voiced consent. "The Khurzan are now considered anarchists threatening Zijikhal prosperity and security. Let it be known!"

Zajid appeared greatly relieved, giving Wellshire an affirmative nod. At last, reason had triumphed over bigotry and fear. Yet as Wellshire gazed out from the pyramid peak at the sprawling city below, he wondered - could prejudice ever truly be purged from society completely?

Over the coming weeks, the elders and Zajid kept Wellshire apprised as sweeping arrests of Khurzan conspirators took place across Zijikhal space. Many fled into hiding at the extremist enclave planets on the outskirts of their territory.

Zajid was hopeful. "Their fangs are pulled, old friend. They become shadows and rumors." He regretted only that their leader had escaped during the citadel attack. "But his hatred consumes him elsewhere now."

Bolstered by this progress, Wellshire requested an audience with the council to plead his full case for reconciliation with the broader galactic community. To his surprise and relief, they granted his petition.

The day of the hearing arrived, and Zajid led Wellshire once more to the towering apex of the central pyramid. The entire council was arranged to receive him. Wellshire steeled his resolve and began speaking from the heart.

He told of humanity's long struggle to overcome its own prejudice and wars. Of the potential for growth when diverse cultures engage with open souls. Of the light that awaits beyond the darkness of fear. The elders listened in contemplative silence to every word.

At last, Wellshire concluded his impassioned plea. "The cosmos holds splendors far beyond any one people's knowledge. But only together may we unlock its deepest secrets."

The head elder was quiet for a long moment before responding. "Wise and courageous words, friend. Perhaps the time has come for our civilization to look outward with new eyes."

Murmurs of agreement rose from the other elders. Zajid appeared deeply moved. This was the culmination of their long efforts. The Zijikhal culture stood on the cusp of a profound realignment.

Yet Wellshire knew the real work was only beginning. Enduring change requires daily effort and empathy. But he had faith these beings could meet the challenge, as humans themselves once had.

Afterwards, as Zajid proudly escorted Wellshire back to his quarters, Wellshire felt a profound sense of hope for the future. There were always obstacles on the road to peace, but perseverance and compassion would light the way.

Chapter 10

Dr. Jessica Middleton gazed up at the cold stars through the cracked visor of the derelict spaceship she now called home. Out here, on a nameless world at the edge of the galaxy, the heavens teemed with possibility and wonder. Yet all she felt was isolation.

It had been three years since the massacre. Three years since the Zijkhal had descended on Calaria, the intellectual heart of the Progenitors' civilization. Three years of fleeing and hiding with the pitiful few thousand survivors. All they had worked towards, gone in two days of fire and death.

During the day, Jessica buried her grief in work, spearheading efforts to rebuild technology in their mountain settlement. But at night, the ghosts returned. Her mentor, Dr. Silva, had first sparked her passion for Xeno-archaeology. Her students who had hung on to her every lecture, their futures obliterated. And Carlos, her dear love Carlos...Gone, like all the rest.

Footsteps outside her cabin door shook Jessica from her brooding. It was Jorall, one of the surviving Progenitor elders, his blue skin wrinkled with weariness. "Pardon the intrusion, Dr. Middleton. The council is assembling for our evening meeting. Shall I inform them you will be delayed?"

Jessica straightened, adjusting her environment suit. "No need, Jorall. I was just reflecting." She grabbed her tablet and headed out into the dusty underground tunnels of the settlement, joining the shuffle of refugees making their way to the central chamber. No time for ghosts tonight.

The twenty remaining Progenitor elders regarded Jessica solemnly as she took her seat at the stone meeting table. Their president, Alora, signaled the start of the meeting. "We have dire matters to discuss tonight. Power reserves approach depletion levels. Food synthesis systems are badly in need of maintenance. Morale is low after yesterday's cave-in."

Murmurs and grim head shakes echoed around the table. They had experienced no shortage of disasters since being forced into hiding. Alora glanced at Jessica. "Dr. Middleton, you mentioned a potential energy source in the nearby mountains?"

Jessica nodded. "Yes, rare mineral deposits that could power a basic fusion reactor for a time. But they're located in extremely treacherous terrain rife with rock worms. We've already lost two scouts trying to survey the region."

Alora sighed heavily, rubbing her temples. "A difficult choice, but we may have no alternatives if our settlement is to endure."

The debate continued late into the night. Risk more lives to power the settlement, or begin rationing to dangerous levels? Each choice seemed to guarantee hardship and death. As despair hung thick in the air, Jorall spoke up.

"President Alora, perhaps we should rethink re-establishing communications." Alora turned on him angrily.

"Don't start this fantasy again. The Zijkhal regime can't be reasoned with!"

Jorall stood firm. "Hear me out. We now believe a small resistance movement has emerged in the city of Zamazaal focused on reform. Perhaps if we started a dialogue."

"After what they've done, you expect negotiation?" Alora cut him off. "You dishonor our dead." Jorall fell silent, eyes downcast. No one dared speak of reconciliation publicly since the massacre. Until now.

Jessica's mind spun as the meeting adjourned. She had lost so much to the Zijkhal. More than anyone would ever know. Contact seemed unthinkable. But late that night, an idea took shape. A slim hope, but hope, nonetheless.

At the next meeting, Jessica hesitantly brought up the Thezan Archives, a vast repository of Progenitor knowledge predating the Zijkhal attacks. "Legends say it remains hidden on a remote outpost world in their territory," she explained to the stunned council.

"Just think, all our lost science, history, culture and perhaps even clues to our origin. If we could recover it, our entire society could be reborn!" Jessica knew she was gambling everything on this long-shot. But she saw a glimmer of hope in the elders' eyes.

After a moment of shocked silence, the room erupted into arguments. It was madness! No, their only hope! Jessica had reignited the tinder of Progenitor aspirations. Perhaps reconciliation need not occur first after all.

For the next week, the settlement was alive with debate over the archives. Scout ships were prepared in secret. Jessica volunteered to pilot the first mission towards Zijkhal space, her heart pounding as launch approached. If she could help resurrect Progenitor civilization, maybe all they had lost would not be in vain. Maybe...just maybe.

Jessica gripped the scout ship's controls tightly as the desolate red planet faded from view. If her calculations were correct, the ruins of Thezan Outpost were less than a week's journey. They were located in a forgotten corner of space far from Zijkhal patrolled routes. She prayed its archives remained intact after all this time.

The small craft slipped into hyperspace, stars blurring into streaks around it. Alone with her thoughts, Jessica's anxieties surfaced. Had she acted rashly, raising expectations about the legends of Thezan? What if the archives held no salvation for her people after all? And how would the Zijkhal react to this violation of their space if discovered?

Still, it was too late for doubts. The survival of the last Progenitors might well hinge on what she found at her mysterious destination. She would land, scout quickly for anything of value, and leave before the Zijkhal were any wiser. Simple, she told herself. Get in, get out.

Approaching the coordinates after several days, Jessica dropped the ship out of hyperspace. A dusty orange world hung in space before her. This was the planet Thezan, if the old charts could be believed. Adjusting course, Jessica descended into the atmosphere.

From high altitude, she scanned the rugged landscape, searching for signs of the outpost. Finally, she spotted a crumbling complex carved into a mesa atop a sheer-faced butte. Jessica carefully set the ship down atop the mesa and suited up before disembarking.

Her boots crunched on the fine dust as she exited the ship. All was still. Gingerly, Jessica approached the nearest collapsed structure, peering into its shadowy depths. Strange symbols marked the eroded walls; this had to be a Progenitor site.

Raising her wrist lamp, Jessica ducked inside. Rubble and twisted metal scattered the floor, but she could make out rooms and corridors extending deeper inside. She followed the ancient passageway farther in, heart racing. There must be a secure archive vault somewhere, but sensors were useless in all this mineral-rich rock.

Several hours passed as Jessica explored the sprawling outpost maze by her wrist lamp's wan glow. At times she would pause, thinking she heard faint scuttling noises in the darkness, but dismissed it as nerves. She was completely alone on this dead world.

Finally, Jessica entered a large chamber that appeared relatively intact. Lining the far wall were rows of intimidating brass doors sealed tight with intricate mechanisms. Stenciled on each in the flowing Progenitor script was a numerical identifier. Vaults!

Rushing over, Jessica examined the nearest vault wheel. It took all her strength to budge the heavy mechanism and open the lock. Pulling the massive door open, she peered inside eagerly, raising her wrist lamp. What ancient wonders awaited rediscovery?

Her shoulders slumped at the sight. Rows of empty shelves and dust. This vault had been stripped clean long ago. Steeling herself, Jessica moved methodically down the row, unsealing and inspecting each chamber. All were similarly bare. No archives, no salvation within their silent walls.

Jessica sank to her knees as despair overwhelmed her. She had failed. The journey, the risks—all for nothing. Their lost past would remain forever buried while the last Progenitors withered away. Only emptiness and darkness awaited them now.

Chapter 11

A sound at the chamber's entrance made Jessica look up with a start. A tall alien figure stood watching her. Definitely not Zijkhal. Luminescent patterns rippled hypnotically across its flowing robes as it stared back with opal eyes. Jessica froze, unable to even reach for her sidearm. What was this being?

Its melodious voice reverberated inside her mind. "I have waited long for one such as you to find this place, Jessica Middleton. We have much to discuss."

Jessica stared wordlessly as the alien glided farther into the vault chamber, robes swirling around its slender frame. She managed to find her voice. "What...what are you? How do you know my name?"

The being's opalescent eyes flashed. "I am called Valtryx. I have watched your journey here from afar." The melodic voice resonated again within Jessica's mind.

"As for what I am, your people knew my kind once, in ages past. We guided them toward knowledge and light. Until conflict scattered us all." A profound sadness entered the alien's tone.

Jessica's heart quickened. Could this being actually have answers about her species' shadowed origins? She rose slowly to face Valtryx. "If you truly know our past, then help me restore what has been lost!"

Valtryx shook his elongated head. "The way back never leads straight. Your archives are now beyond physical reach." Jessica's excitement crumbled back into despair at those words.

But Valtryx continued. "The Zijkhal plundered this place long ago. But all knowledge merely seeds more insight in time. What matters dwells not in artifacts, but within." He tapped a long, slender finger to his temple meaningfully.

Jessica's scientific mind raced, struggling to interpret his cryptic words. Valtryx drew closer, aura rippling hypnotically. "Your peoples' destinies are still entwined, though past pain obscures this. The Zijkhal too once understood but fell far."

Hope and confusion warred within Jessica. "Please, just tell me plainly. We've suffered enough riddles!" Unexpected sympathy entered the alien's resonant voice. "You shall have plain truth, though it lays bare difficult roads ahead."

Valtryx waved a hand and reality itself seemed to ripple. Jessica gasped as a vast cosmic vista expanded before her, nebulae and galaxies swirling by faster than light. Valtryx guided the vision to a DNA helix unraveling and re-coiling endlessly.

"All life is connected. The Market hums, and we sense its echoes." Jessica's consciousness reeled at his words and the incomprehensible scale of what she was seeing. DNA wove itself into Zijkhal, Progenitors, and countless more species

As suddenly as it began, the vision collapsed back to the empty vault. Jessica steadied herself against a shelf, overwhelmed. Valtryx's voice was firm but comforting. "Your two peoples diverged long ago but must reunite. Only together may your true legacy be claimed."

His form began glowing brighter, as if about to dematerialize. "Go now and plant seeds of understanding. In time, they shall bear wondrous fruit." Valtryx eyed Jessica intently as he faded from view. "Trust in the patterns..."

Then Jessica found herself alone again in the dark chamber. She blinked, wondering if she had hallucinated it all. But no—etched on the vault floor where Valtryx had stood was a single glowing symbol. Some kind of dowsing device? A map? Its meaning escaped her.

With no archives left to uncover, Jessica made her way back to the ship in a daze, the strange sign burning in her mind. Though the mission had failed, she now carried something far more valuable—a glimpse of cosmic connectedness binding all life, even Progenitors and Zijkhal.

The vision changed everything. No matter how impossible or dangerous, communication had to be opened between their peoples as Valtryx urged. The symbol's meaning would become clear in time. Jessica resolved that, against all odds, understanding must prevail.

As the scout ship lifted off from the Thezan Outpost, Jessica set course not back to the hidden settlement, but towards Zijkhal space. She would find the reform movement Jorall had spoken of and bridge this divide somehow. The first step was one of faith. Jessica watched the stars stream by, no longer feeling alone in the vastness.

Jessica knew convincing the other Progenitors to open communication with the Zijkhal would be no easy task after years of displacement and hardship. But the mystical encounter with Valtryx had awakened something deep within, a sense of destiny that defied logic or caution. She had to try.

Upon returning to the hidden settlement, Jessica requested an emergency council meeting. The elders listened in disturbed silence as she recounted her experience on the Thezan Outpost and Valtryx's revelations. Dismayed murmurs arose after she finished her account.

"This is deeply troubling," President Alora said gravely. "We sent you to recover the archives, not consume alien hallucinations." The others voiced their agreement.

Jessica pleaded with them to see reason. "What if Valtryx spoke the truth about our connected past? We turned away from reconciliation once; let us not make the same mistake again."

The debate raged late into the night. In the end, the council refused to condone contacting the Zijkhal without concrete evidence. Respect for Jessica led them to delay informing others about her inexplicable visions for now. But she was forbidden from pursuing the matter any further.

Jessica, however, would not be deterred. After days of soul-searching, she came to realize the glowing symbol Valtryx had left represented coordinates, likely for a Zijkhal reformer outpost. She would seek them out, with or without the council's approval.

In the dead of night, Jessica slipped away to a scout ship docked on the settlement's periphery. She input the coordinates from memory and launched into space, the old vessel rumbling under her. Let them call her mad. She embraced that title now for the sake of peace.

It was a long and lonely journey to the coordinates. Jessica had no idea what awaited at her destination—capture or salvation, friend or foe. But she had faith this was the course Valtryx intended her to follow. She watched the traverse lines on the navigation display slowly converge as she neared the mysterious location.

Emerging from hyperspace, Jessica beheld an asteroid belt strewn with jagged planetoids. Scanners detected hollowed-out structures and energy signatures consistent with habitation. This seemed to be the place. Silently, she slipped the scout ship into the tumbling field of rocks.

Weaving between icy crags, Jessica followed the energy traces to a large asteroid pocked with silvery domes and antennae. There was no indication whether this outpost was friendly or hostile. Holding course, she approached what looked like a docking bay entrance.

A voice crackled over the comm in gruff Zijkhal. "Unidentified vessel, you trespass on grounds of the Intercession Movement. State your purpose at once." Jessica froze—this was the moment of truth.

Heart pounding, she opened the channel. "My name is Jessica Middleton. I am...from earth. I was visiting the Progenitors and escaped with a few thousand refugees." Only stunned silence followed her words. "I have come unarmed and alone. Please, allow me to land so we may talk of reconciliation."

After an agonizing silence, coordinates flashed on her console directing Jessica to a landing area within the asteroid base. She had taken the first immense step. Whatever fate awaited inside, she was ready. The scout ship touched down gently. Taking a deep breath, Jessica unsealed the hatch and stepped out.

Two Zijkhal in simple gray robes awaited her solemnly on the smooth metallic floor. "Come with us. Zajid will want to meet you without delay." Jessica followed the robed Zijkhal through a maze of corridors carved into the asteroid's heart. There was no going back now.

At last, they entered a circular chamber glowing with strange pillars of light. Another Zijkhal dressed in humble attire turned to face Jessica in surprise. "The Progenitor lives? How can this be?" Jessica recognized genuine shock and wonder in his expression.

"My survival does seem impossible," she acknowledged. "But perhaps it was meant to be. Are you Zajid, the one who seeks reform?" The Zijkhal nodded slowly, looking over Jessica as if she were an apparition. "Then let us talk of our peoples' past, and future."

For hours, Jessica related the Progenitors' long exile and near-extinction by the Zijkhal armada. Zajid told of the first Zijkhal reformers and their struggles to spread empathy and nonviolence. Both had journeyed far down arduous roads.

"But now fate allows us to unite where once we were divided," Zajid observed, placing a clawed hand gently on Jessica's shoulder. She knew then this was the beginning of a shared destiny foreseen by Valtryx. Much hardship lay ahead, but together, reconciliation was possible against any odds.

After parting ways with Valtryx, Jessica Middleton boarded the sleek Progenitor spacecraft provided for her return to Earth. Though antiquated, the ship's metastable shields and tachyon drive core enabled interstellar leaps a modern human vessel could scarcely dream of. Jessica sat at the intricate control interface, unsure of what awaited her upon returning after so long away.

Following the cryptic navigation path Valtryx had transferred, Jessica set course for Earth. The memories of her past life there now felt centuries distant after walking so long among the stars. The culture and politics of now-alien Earth held little meaning for her anymore. Yet somewhere on her homeworld were answers to the Progenitors' exile that could prove vital to the future.

The dusty archives and clandestine contacts Jessica had left behind so long ago were her only link to unraveling the truth. Trusting Valtryx's guidance, she had no clear idea yet where this lonely quest would lead. As Earth's familiar sun grew closer, Jessica steeled herself for the strangeness awaiting her upon returning to everything once known.

As the sleek spacecraft Valtryx had provided emerged from its final jump, Earth's familiar sun came into view ahead. Jessica watched her homeworld grow larger in the viewport, conflicted feelings rising within. She had walked strange eons since her time there long ago. What did the Earth hold for her now?

Jessica wondered if the archives and clandestine contacts she left behind still existed. So much time had passed; would anyone remember the quiet historian who vanished mysteriously? She braced herself for a cold trail or worse.

Flashes of memory surfaced unbidden—her cramped university office piled high with ancient texts, longing gazes at the Hypatia's off-limits modules, the heart-pounding night she stole the Meridian files. That fateful moment had set her life on an unbelievable trajectory far beyond any dream.

Piercing the outer atmosphere, Jessica saw the familiar continents come into focus through wispy clouds. Since her departure, generations had come and gone there. From high above, nothing seemed to have changed across the endless cycles. Yet Jessica knew in her bones the gulf separating her from the world below was profound.

Angling towards the secluded coordinates Valtryx provided, Jessica spotted the Meridian sanctuary nestled discreetly in a rugged wilderness. The cloaking systems accepted her approach code, revealing a concealed landing area within a rocky basin. Jessica set the spacecraft down gracefully, taking a steadying breath. The time had come to see what secrets Earth still held.

Chapter 12

Wellshire gazed out the towering pyramid's window as the Zijkhal capital bustled below. Months had passed since the elders publicly condemned the violent Khurzan faction. While tensions persisted, day to day life in the citadel seemed peaceful on the surface. But Wellshire wondered, did acceptance truly take root, or prejudice still linger silently?

A knock at his chamber door interrupted Wellshire's reflection. He turned to see Zajid enter, wearing an expression both troubled and hopeful.

"My friend, astonishing news has arrived that may change everything," Zajid said. "Come, we must speak in true privacy." Intrigued, Wellshire followed him through the maze of inner passages known only to Zajid.

They emerged atop a secluded tower overlooking the capital. Zajid checked their surroundings carefully before speaking in a hushed tone.

"I have received encrypted communication from our outpost in the Small Magellanic Cloud. A lone Progenitor has made contact." He let those shocking words sink in. Wellshire struggled to grasp their implications. One Progenitor still lived? How was it possible?

Zajid related the full message detailing the encounter. "Her intentions seem sincere. She speaks of reconciliation, of hidden connected pasts between our kinds." He searched Wellshire's face for a reaction.

Wellshire's mind reeled. After long believing the Progenitors annihilated, could reunion with even one survivor heal these bleeding wounds in history? He turned to Zajid resolutely.

"We must bring her here, share this revelation with the council. If any ember of hope for true peace remains, we must kindle it to light." Zajid nodded firmly in agreement. There was much to be done.

Wellshire chose to keep knowledge of the development limited for now. The surviving Progenitor's arrival must be managed with wisdom and care. Confronting the elders too suddenly could provoke volatile reactions before empathy took root.

Instead, he focused his energies on gently steering conversations with key elder statesmen, philosophers and historians toward receptiveness and openness. Meanwhile, Zajid secretly arranged safe transport from the outpost.

During this time, Wellshire continued his public engagements promoting values of nonviolence and interconnection. "Change rarely occurs overnight. Hearts and minds must be coaxed along steadily." Occasionally he caught glimpses of Khurzan sympathizers lurking on the peripheries, their presence a reminder of lingering darkness.

At last, the fateful day arrived. Zajid discreetly informed Wellshire preparations were complete to receive the Progenitor visitor. She would land that evening at a secured rooftop platform. Wellshire could scarcely concentrate, consumed with curiosity and questions about this mysterious survivor.

When twilight fell over the citadel, Wellshire and Zajid ascended to the concealed landing area and waited anxiously. Minutes stretched on, until a sleek cloaked shuttle suddenly decloaked before them. The hatch spiraled open, and a figure appeared.

For a moment, Wellshire saw not a Progenitor, but only another weary soul, scarred by loss, sustained by hope. He stepped forward and extended his hand in welcome. "I am called Wellshire. What is your name, friend?"

She regarded him solemnly with azure eyes. "My name is Valra." Zajid bowed his head respectfully beside Wellshire. "Then we bid you welcome, Valra. Let the healing begin."

The three stood in silence as the lights of the Zijkhal capital shimmered below. Though a difficult road lay ahead, in this moment, all could feel the first fragile strands of understanding taking root between them.

Valra followed Wellshire and Zajid into a spacious chamber deep within the central pyramid. Her pulse quickened as she gazed at the alien furnishings and architectural flourishes so unlike anything a Progenitor would design. She was truly immersed in Zijkhal civilization now, the first of her kind to venture here peacefully in ages.

Wellshire gestured for Valra to make herself comfortable on an ornate chair. "I know you must be weary from your long journey. Please, relax and eat." He indicated a platter of exotic fruit on the table beside her.

Valra selected a reddish oval fruit and sampled it. Sweet nectar filled her mouth, mingling with a strange tingling spice.

Before she realized it, she had devoured the entire fruit, suddenly aware of how famished she was.

Wellshire's projected face radiated satisfaction. "I'm pleased to see you enjoying our j'nara fruit. May it nourish both body and spirit." He sat down opposite her. "Now, please tell us your extraordinary tale, Valra. However impossible, I know it must be true."

Haltingly at first, then with increasing fluidity, Valra opened up about her civilization's tragic downfall, their survival by wit and resilience, and the mystical experience that set her on this journey. Wellshire and Zajid listened silently, though she sensed their horror and sympathy.

As she recounted meeting Valtryx and the revelation of cosmic connectedness between their peoples, Wellshire's floating facial features furrowed pensively. Valra finished her tale and sat back, suddenly drained. Just telling it had reawakened that maelstrom of emotions.

Zajid spoke solemnly. "You honor us with your trust despite past pain. We shall do all in our power to forge a new path forward together." He glanced at Wellshire keenly. "When do you propose informing the elders? This changes everything."

Wellshire steepled his fingers, lost in thought. "Let her presence be unveiled gradually, organically. Those clinging to old prejudice must be given time to reflect before minds unclench." He addressed Valra warmly. "For now, you should rest from your travels."

Valra nodded, feeling the full weight of exhaustion now that her tale was told. There would be much more discussion ahead. As she settled in to sleep in the adjacent chamber, Valra felt the first glimmers of hope about her people's future, so long mired in despair. Perhaps this was the lifeline they had unknowingly awaited.

Over the next several days, Valra acquainted herself with the innermost sanctums of the great pyramid under Wellshire and Zajid's guidance. Each night they shared engaging conversation, slowly unraveling the tangled histories that had led to so much bloodshed. Valra found herself mesmerized by Zijkhal art and culture.

Meanwhile, word of a mysterious foreign dignitary visiting the upper echelons of the pyramid quietly began circulating in the capital. Curiosity mounted, but Wellshire remained vague about the visitor's identity to allow anticipation to build. The time to bridge this divide publicly was drawing near.

When curiosity reached fever pitch, Wellshire requested a special assembly of the council, Zajid and Valra atop the pyramid peak under the open sun. As they ascended toward the bright platform, Valra's heart pounded. This was it, the moment of reconciliation. Thousands of years of painful history hinged on this meeting. She murmured a quiet prayer.

The elders' assemblage regarded Valra with naked shock as she was introduced. After so much loss, hope was almost impossible to bear. Yet here was a living Progenitor before them, extending the hand of fellowship. One by one, they embraced her in the traditional Zijkhal manner. Some could not restrain their tears.

As they settled around the stone table, Valra saw the bustling capital spread out below, oblivious to this moment. Turning back, she related her tale again to the transfixed council. Hope burgeoned anew in each elder's heart as her impossible account unfolded. Here was a chance to chart a new course at last.

When Valra finished, she extended her open hands to the elders. "Let the past remain buried, so our children may know life." The eldest councilor rose solemnly and clasped her hands in his clawed ones with deep reverence.

"You honor us beyond words with your wisdom and courage. At last, let the darkness be lifted so our peoples may unite." One by one, each elder joined hands with her until all were connected. A new era had begun.

After Valra's arrival, remarkable changes swept the Zijkhal capital. Inspired by her act of trust, more citizens began questioning old prejudices and seeking facts over whatever fit their bias. Wellshire redoubled his efforts connecting with community groups to share knowledge through compassionate dialogue.

Meanwhile, Valra and Wellshire worked closely to slowly illuminate the full truth of their peoples' connected pasts. Historians were consulted, archives unsealed, and lively academic debates held publicly for the first time. Pieces long forgotten were woven into a nuanced tapestry.

Day by day, curiosity overcame fear as the populace learned just how intertwined Zijkhal and Progenitor destiny had been under the ancestors. United once, sundered by audacity, the cosmos now gifted a chance to reforge wholeness from fragments.

During this cultural reawakening, Valra often gazed across the capitol from the pyramid's pinnacle, taking strength from watching barriers dissolve. She transmitted encrypted messages to the hidden Progenitor settlement, urging them to reconsider contact. The responses grew less resistant in time.

Of course, prejudice died hard for some. Valra was accustomed to wary stares when visiting lower streets on her walks with Wellshire. Occasionally they glimpsed shadowy figures stalking behind, only to dart away when noticed.

Hardline Khurzan loyalists still posed an ever-present danger. But their bitterness seemed increasingly irrelevant as most Zijkhal awakened to possibility. The future looked brighter by the day.

One azure evening, Valra and Wellshire were approached by an elder statesman named Zanthor seeking an urgent council with them. His face was grim as he led them to a sealed chamber.

"My friends, I am afraid a threat has arisen that cannot be ignored," Zanthor rasped. "Shortly after your arrival, Valra, a Shapeshifter scarlet force of Khurzan extremists, secretly left the capital. They mean to find the Progenitor settlement and finish the old work."

Valra's heart turned to ice. All the good beginnings here could be utterly undone if the survivors were massacred. Wellshire's projected face furrowed with concern. "Do you know their destination?"

Zanthor shook his head. "Our knowledge is limited. But we have dispatched covert tracker scouts to pursue their vapor trails and warn your people. You must send an envoy to coordinate defenses!"

Valra's mind raced. This would require returning to convince the skeptical council she once abandoned. But the colonists' lives hung in the balance. Turning to Zanthor, she responded firmly. "Then an envoy you shall have. Ready a ship immediately."

Wellshire placed a supportive hand on Valra's shoulder. "Your bravery humbles me, dear friend. May your people at last see past fear to the future that unites us all." Nodding silently, Valra set off to gather Wellshire's message of reconciliation and warning. She only prayed it would not come too late.

The sleek Zijkhal scout vessel slipped into the blackness of space, racing towards Progenitor space. Inside, Valra prepared herself for the coming confrontation. Making the elders see reason against old prejudice would be an uphill battle, even with a genocidal force en route. Time was terribly short.

But Valra knew in her soul this darkness too would pass if met with courage. She would make them understand somehow, just as she had seen beyond her own hatred those months ago. Valra watched the traverse lines converge, hurtling towards destiny. The cosmos itself seemed to be holding its breath, waiting.

The council of Progenitor elders reacted with shock and outrage when Valra appeared unannounced to warn of the extremist threat. She pleaded with them to put aside fear and mistrust for survival's sake.

"You conspire with those who butchered our families, then dare ask us to flee into their arms?" Alora said bitterly, glaring at Valra. "We will defend what little remains with our last breath."

Valra struggled to make them understand. "I once harbored the same hatred. But these Zijkhal risked all to warn us, believing reconciliation possible." Still the council refused to budge, voting to force Valra into solitary quarantine for collusion.

That night, alone in her locked chamber with a desperation born of love, Valra hacked the colony network using old credentials. She transmitted a video message directly to all citizens, relating the imminent danger and chance to break the cycle of violence at last. "Have faith in each other," she urged them. "Darkness cannot persist in open hearts."

The next morning, chaos gripped the council as crowds gathered outside demanding dialogue with the Zijkhal envoy. Valra's appeal had touched souls weary of fear and loss. At last Alora relented, allowing Wellshire's message of hope to be broadcast colony wide.

Wellshire's gentle eloquence moved the Progenitors profoundly. As if a curtain was drawn back to reveal long-obscured light, the people recognized their own pain and fears mirrored in the Zijkhal. How long had they kept each other bound in the shadows? Could they dare believe redemption was possible?

But deep mistrust still simmered in some elders' hearts. The vote to establish communication remained deadlocked late into the night. Until Joral, who had first proposed outreach what seemed a lifetime ago, quietly changed his stance. "For our children's future, my friend," he said to Valra. "Let us be brave."

The critical decision made, Progenitor and Zijkhal Envoy vessels met discreetly in space. Valra greeted Wellshire with tearful relief. "Your words touched hearts long hardened. But dark days are still ahead." Together, they began coordinating the colony's desperate evacuation to Zijkhal sanctuary.

A tense exodus took place under the looming threat of Khurzan arrival. Most Progenitors chose to flee into exile rather than stand and fight. Each ship that lifted away bearing refugees felt like a hopeful victory, though abandoning their settlement wounded deeply.

The evacuation was nearing completion when Zanthor's scouts sent an emergency alert. The Khurzan warships had entered the system on an extermination course. With no time to lose, the last colonial transports broke orbit under Zijkhal escort just as the enemy force emerged from hyperspace.

Valra watched from Wellshire's ship as the abandoned Progenitor settlement below erupted into flame and debris under the Khurzan barrage. Though now empty, seeing their last foothold obliterated stung them bitterly. Valra turned away, whispering a prayer for the lost. Wellshire embraced her in solemn silence.

Slipping quietly away, the survivors made the long journey to a Zijkhal sanctuary. An uncertain future awaited, but united now against hatred, Valra and Wellshire stood ready to greet it together. They would mourn, rebuild, and continue until their peoples were healed at last. This was only the beginning.

When the weary Progenitor convoy finally arrived, the Zijkhal welcomed them with gifts of fruit and flowers tolling bells of celebration. Valra stepped off onto the spaceport amidst the crowd and stopped a Zijkhal child gazing at her in wonderment. "Go in peace, little one," she said softly. "This world is for you now."

Chapter 13

The Zijkhal capital's winding streets thrummed with activity as inhabitants of all ages went about their lives. Eight cycles had passed since the Progenitor refugees arrived, and a sense of unity unlike any before permeated the great citadel.

Where distrust had choked the unreconciled past, former enemies now walked together under blossoming trees that honored the many new beginnings nurtured to fruition. Though much healing was still needed, hope flourished.

In the central plaza, Progenitor and Zijkhal children laughed together joyfully, the ancient divide now a relic of history class to them. Seeing youths of two peoples form bonds that would have been unthinkable not long ago, Valra felt seeds planted long ago coming into bloom.

Rising from the bench where she had paused to enjoy the plaza's cheer, Valra continued on her way to meet Wellshire at the embassy. Since the refugees arrived, he had spearheaded great cultural reconciliation through his gift of communication.

Wellshire's wisdom reminded Valra that true change takes time and persistence. Old conflicts cast long shadows not dispelled in a day. Yet seeing the city's harmony gave her faith.

Arriving at the open, glass-domed structure that now served as a joint Progenitor-Zijkhal diplomatic center, Valra took a lift up to Wellshire's office and was surprised to find Zajid already there. His expression was deeply serious.

"What has happened?" Valra asked. The two had served as her dearest friends since that first fateful contact. Zajid sighed heavily in his gravelly voice. "Come, let us speak where no other ears may hear."

Valra followed them to the privacy of the rooftop sanctuary garden. Wellshire turned to her, projected face clouded with concern. "I am afraid we have received disturbing reports from the outer colonies. Our newfound unity is still fragile there."

Zajid clenched a clawed fist. "Khurzan sympathizers are stirring up anti-Progenitor sentiments again. They falsely claim your people are exploiting old weaknesses to seize control."

Valra felt as if the ground dropped away. She thought the violent ideology banished after the survivors were welcomed. "I will go there myself and make this right," she said firmly. "Our peoples have sacrificed too much for the future to let darkness drive us apart."

Wellshire nodded solemnly. "I hoped you would offer, my friend. Your wisdom and courage have become a light during difficult times. But the journey will not be easy." Their people's reconciliation still balanced upon a razor's edge. Much depended on Valra's faith and vision.

She placed her hands over both of theirs. "When has that ever stopped me before? We will make this journey together." Wellshire and Zajid bowed their heads, honoring her steadfast spirit. Though the road ahead was fraught with uncertainty, each knew their cause was just.

After hastily arranging affairs and recording messages of support to broadcast, Valra boarded a diplomatic starship bound for the fractious colonies. Wellshire and Zajid stood together watching its silvery form rise and vanish into the clouds, carrying the embodiment of all they had sacrificed for across the stars.

Valra gazed out the cockpit as the planet faded from view, bound on her new mission of reconciliation. Though she had not expected unrest to resurface so soon, the colonists' confusion and fear could surely be calmed through compassionate reason. She only prayed she was not too late. The long traverse to the outer worlds loomed before her, but she did not feel alone. Their people's hopes traveled with her.

Settling in for the long journey, Valra poured over the reports detailing the unrest. The tide of public opinion in the colonies had turned sharply. Rumors spread that Progenitor refugees were infiltrating institutions and gathering data to help a takeover. Clearly absurd, but suspicion fanned by zealots rarely bowed to facts.

She would need to meet the instigators' dishonesty head-on with honesty and trust. As Wellshire taught, darkness can't persist with hope. These colonies' fears stemmed from pain she knew intimately. By opening her heart fearlessly, theirs would follow. It was the only way forward.

The ship slipped into hyperspace in a flash of particles, stars blurring to ribbons around it. Valra watched the shimmering traverse lines creep steadily toward their convergence. Each minute carried her closer to the latest trial awaiting their peoples. But whatever happened, she would face it without compromise or hesitation. Too much depended on it now.

The starship dropped out of hyperspace as the dusty orange sphere of Colony 32 loomed into view. Valra steadied herself, preparing to disembark and confront the unrest threatening to undo years of reconciliation.

Reports showed anti-Progenitor sentiment was strongest in the capital, fueled by rumors and insecurity. Valra's mission was to face it directly with an appeal to unity and reason. But radicals stoking fear would not make it easy.

Descending through wispy rust-colored clouds, Valra caught her first glimpse of the sprawling colony city. It reminded her of archival images of old Progenitor settlements in design. But time had worn its gleaming edges, matching the weary caution hardening its resident's hearts.

The ship touched down gently in a carved stone plaza before the central governance tower. As the hatch hissed open, Valra was surprised to find elder councilors already waiting to receive her. She had expected aloof formality, yet their body language radiated warm welcome.

"Emissary Valra, your bravery honors us," one said, clasping her hands in the traditional greeting. "Forgive those among us clinging to the past. Fear makes children of elders." Hope flickered in Valra's chest. Change was already underway.

After an exchange of respectful formalities, the elders escorted Valra into the tower to meet the ruling Prime Consul. He appeared exhausted from balancing stability and unrest. But seeing Valra rekindled a weary smile.

"Your presence brings much needed wisdom in this trying time. Come, let us speak plainly." He ushered her to his private chambers away from any listening ears. Here, true hearts could be unlocked.

As they settled around a stone table etched with intricate scrollwork, the Prime Consul shook his head solemnly. "A splinter faction has seized upon old fears, willfully blind to how far we have come together. But many stand ready to follow your lead."

Valra leaned forward, meeting his eyes with earnest intensity. "Then help me reach them. Lend your voice to call for open assembly where truth may be spoken and heard." The Prime Consul considered thoughtfully, then nodded. "So shall it be."

That night, the Prime Consul broadcast an announcement throughout the city inviting all citizens to gather at sunrise in the great amphitheater. There, he assured them, questions would be addressed and understanding fostered. Valra prayed open hearts would come looking for light.

The next morning Valra awaited the assembly with nervous anticipation. As citizens filed into the stone amphitheater, she scanned their varied faces, reminded of the shared hopes that transcended appearances. When the Prime Consul opened the floor to her, she stepped forward.

Valra's voice rang out clear and true as she related the long road walked together with former enemies now turned friends. Rumors shattered against bedrock truth as she recalled the Refuge and Reconciliation accords. Fears dimmed under her account of children of both peoples playing joyfully together.

When Valra finished, she extended her hand openly in friendship. The amphitheater fell silent in thought. Then, an elder worker came forth and clasped it warmly. "For the hope of our children," he said. One by one, more joined hands until a circle of understanding united all. Much work remained, but a corner was turned.

That evening, the Prime Consul celebrated unity with a great feast. Valra saw former adversaries laughing together under garlands of local flowers and knew this harvest flowed from seeds planted in compassion long ago. There would be lapses and doubts again, but love would lead them through.

As Valra prepared to leave the next day, crowds lined the streets to bid her farewell, waving banners hand-painted with messages of hope and fellowship. The elders embraced her, expressing profound gratitude for her coming. They would continue the work, no longer beguiled by those looking to divide. Watching the colony recede into the stars, Valra was filled with faith in the future they would build together.

The sleek starship glided silently through space as Valra returned from her successful reconciliation mission. Though much work remained, she had made significant progress calming fears and renewing purpose in the colony's inhabitants. Dark voices would always threaten unity, but she was confident compassion would prevail over them.

As the planet where her new life had truly begun grew closer, Valra's thoughts turned to Bitty. The young Zijkhal child she had bonded closely with these past cycles would be overjoyed at her homecoming. Bitty's innocence in befriending a former enemy deeply moved Valra, a tender shoot sprouting in the ashes of war's bitterness.

Approaching the shimmering sphere swirled with clouds, Valra felt her pulse quicken. Scanning the spaceport launch control frequencies, she requested landing clearance, hoping to surprise Wellshire and Zajid. The journey had drained her, but sweet reunion lay ahead.

The sleek ship pierced the stratosphere and angled toward the sprawling capital. Valra gazed upon the mosaic of glass and metal comprising the great citadel, marveling that structures birthed in shared purpose had replaced the rubble of collapsed enmity. This sacred ground nourished all who opened their hearts to it.

With a whisper-soft touchdown amidst spaceport traffic, the starship completed its long voyage. Valra swiftly completed post-flight checks and shouldered her essential items. As the hatch spiraled open, the mingled scents of the city greeted her - so unlike the recycled starship environment she had become acclimated to. It was good to be back under open skies.

Weaving her way through the bustling spaceport, Valra relished being immersed in the energetic crowds of citizens from both peoples going about their lives in unity. Eight cycles ago, such a scene would have seemed unimaginable. Every smiling face, each simple act of living, spoke to the hard-won trust now taken almost for granted.

Outside the spaceport, Valra turned along a tree-lined footpath leading into the heart of the central district. Halfway along its length, one tree caught her eye. Its trunk was engraved intricately with Progenitor and Zijkhal symbols entwined together. Pausing, Valra was struck by how organically reconciliation had taken root in this new generation.

Further along, Valra found herself drawn to a vibrant public square where Zijkhal and Progenitor adolescents socialized freely, laughing together without reservation or strangeness. A park bench bore a dedication plaque: 'May old walls crumble so all may know belonging.' Smiling softly, Valra resumed her way.

Rounding a corner, Valra spotted the familiar crystalline facade of the reconciliation embassy where Wellshire presided. Her pace quickened, eager to reunite with her dearest friends and share all that had occurred. A new day was dawning for their peoples, but true peace demanded continued devotion. Much growth lay ahead, but no longer need it be walked alone under cold stars. Together, they were home.

Wellshire's projected face lit up with surprise and delight when Valra appeared unexpectedly at the embassy entrance. "Dear friend, you have returned! We did not expect you for some time yet." He embraced her warmly in the traditional manner.

Valra smiled, relishing Wellshire's gentle wisdom which had meant so much since her arrival. "The ancestors blessed our efforts. Minds unclenched and hope prevailed." She went on to relate the details of her reconciliation mission to the colony.

Wellshire's shimmering gaze grew thoughtful as he listened intently. "Your compassion and courage shine as a beacon for us all, Valra. Come, Zajid will be most pleased by your swift success." He led her within while contacting Zajid.

Zajid arrived in short order, gravelly voice rumbling with laughter as he enfolded Valra in an affectionate embrace. "Ah, once again you exceed expectations! Your light spurs all to nobler heights." Valra bowed graciously, warmed by her friends' pride.

The three spent the next hours in joyful conversation, reminiscing on the long road walked together. From tentative first contact, to an unimaginable leap of trust, their actions had gradually dissolved the barriers separating their peoples. There had been setbacks and trials yet love prevailed over fear.

Later, as crimson twilight fell over the citadel, Valra set out to reconnect with the city she had left weeks prior. Though away guiding others, her spirit had remained here where a new world was taking shape. She had much to rediscover after her travels.

The plazas, streets, and winding footpaths all seemed imbued with new energy and purpose. Citizens went about their lives with an easy solidarity that spoke to old hatreds fading. There was still far to go, but the foundation was strong.

Pausing on a secluded footbridge overlooking the central district, Valra was enraptured by the dance of colored lights outside the commerce halls and homes. Once these gleaming towers had stood uniform and bare, now their inhabitants adorned them with beauty reflecting the prosperity within. Life flourished in this new age.

Wandering aimlessly, letting the vibrant spirit of her adoptive city reconnect with her soul, Valra found herself carried back to the quiet square containing the memorial to old walls fallen. Here, more than anywhere, the promise of what their peoples might achieve together was given form. Valra sat upon the inscribed bench, reflecting on all who had sacrificed to gift this future. The night air was rich with hope.

Chapter 14

The capital awoke to an uncertain new day. During the night cycle, a garbled transmission of unknown origin had infiltrated all communication channels. Though lasting only seconds, the cryptic fragments felt like a dark omen:

"...the fire shall purge..."

"...death to the old order..."

"...Khurzan rises again..."

Concerned murmurs rippled through the city as citizens gathered to discuss the odd occurrence. No authority had issued any statement yet. Wild speculation abounded in the absence of facts.

Valra hurried to the diplomatic embassy where an emergency council had been called. Wellshire's projections bore a grim look she had not seen since the refugees arrived. He nodded solemnly as Valra entered and took her seat.

"My friends...we all know what darkness this harbors," Wellshire began, his voice uncharacteristically heavy. "I had hoped we would never hear these venomous whispers again. But it seems hate festers still in unseen corners."

The council radiated a tense anxiety. After so much progress, the ghosts of Khurzan fanaticism returned to haunt them. Valra spoke up as the terrible silence lingered. "We must not jump to conclusions until the source is found. Fear only aids our enemies." The elders murmured agreement, buoyed by her rational courage.

After much debate, it was agreed to dispatch covert inspectors to the outer colonies while officially downplaying the transmission for now. If extremists were regrouping, secrecy remained critical. The council adjourned, fearing the worst but still clinging to fragile hope.

In the days that followed, a sense of uncertainty gripped the capital as rumors multiplied wildly. Minor incidents sparked protests and vandalism between groups quick to blame old enemies. Valra worked tirelessly with Wellshire to temper the unrest, but unity fraying rapidly.

Strange malfunctions increased across vital systems. Food and water synthesizers would inexplicably fail, spawn erratic results, or shut down entirely. Technicians discovered tampering but no culprits. Wary distrust returned to poison the community lifeblood so vital to sustaining the peace.

Valra reached out to her contacts in the outer colonies only to find similar patterns of sabotage and provocation surfacing. Few leads materialized as these invisible forces coalesced to fray society's bonds. Each passing day carried more ominous news.

When the primary power grid flickered and failed temporarily, plunging half the capital into darkness, public anxiety turned to anger and open conflict. Valra desperately pleaded for nonviolence, but enmity refused to be contained.

Under the emergency dome of temporary light Wellshire activated over the embassy, Valra confronted the painful truth—Khurzan had risen from the ashes. Somehow their toxins had seeped silently into society's cracks to spread division anew. All she and so many others had built now tottered dangerously. But Valra knew with absolute conviction that hope would endure somehow, until light purified all shadows. Gripped by smoldering determination, she began planning her response. Khurzan's dark fire would not claim this future.

Valra hastily convened an emergency meeting with Wellshire and Zajid as chaos threatened to consume the capital. She paced under the shimmering diplomatic shield Wellshire was exerting to protect the embassy.

"Friends, our worst fears have come to pass. Khurzan's poison has already deeply infected our cities," Valra said grimly.

Zajid snarled in frustration. "And yet the cowards hide in shadows! No one claims these vile acts." He slammed a fist on the stone table.

Wellshire's projections flickered with concern. "Darkness prefers anonymity. But we must not let panic take root."

Valra stopped and met their eyes. "You speak wisely, Wellshire. Fear makes more fear. We need facts to combat these lies." She activated a scanner module, searching for signs of surveillance. Finding none, she leaned in close.

"I propose a mission to infiltrate and follow traces of Khurzan activity back to the source. Are you with me?"

Zajid nodded without hesitation. "I would tear limb from limb those who threaten our future."

Wellshire considered thoughtfully. "A dangerous path...yet perhaps necessary. You have my support, dear friends."

Their course decided, the three began laying plans in utmost secrecy. They identified likely vectors of Khurzan influence using activity patterns and psychological profiles.

Wellshire tapped into surveillance feeds, seeing signs of organized sabotage hidden amidst growing unrest.

Valra reached out to trusted contacts in the colonies, urging them to quietly seek out groups speaking of renewed racial purity and old ways. Zajid secured false identities and encrypted communicators.

As the capital's stability deteriorated, their window of opportunity was closing. Two cycles later, all preparations were complete. Valra hugged Bitty tightly, hating to leave without explanation. Zajid bade his offspring farewell in their sacred manner. Wellshire removed traces of their plans from all systems. This secret campaign began.

Slipping away in the night, Valra and Zajid made their way through chaotic streets towards the predetermined infiltration point—a dissenter meeting in the warehouse district.

Valra pulled up the hood of her cloak, disguising her Progenitor features. Zajid peeled a biomimetic film over himself, assuming the appearance of a radical Zijkhal. They exchanged one last steadying look and melted into the shadows.

The coded entry system accepted their fake identities, and they descended into the tense, dimly lit gathering. Furtive figures muttered amongst themselves, anger palpable beneath the surface.

Valra cautiously broached conversation with a hooded Zijkhal hiding in the periphery. "Brother, what word from the outer worlds?"

His response chilled her. "The roots nourished by noble sacrifice grow strong in secret...the day of renewal approaches."

Their worst fears were confirmed. Khurzan had metastasized like a cancer.

For two tense cycles, Valra and Zajid infiltrated meetings, slowly tracing tendrils of coded communications, plans, propaganda materials and explosives. But the radicals took extreme precautions to prevent exposure. Each discovery still left them far from the epicenter.

Until late one night, an encrypted data vault yielded a vital clue: a navigation beacon signal path used by inner circle messengers. Valra and Zajid quickly decrypted the signal and pursued it into space toward a remote system scarred by ancient battles. The hunt for Khurzan's hidden architects would now begin in earnest.

The dusty red planet loomed large in the viewport as Valra and Zajid's sleek cloaked ship slipped silently into high orbit. According to the encrypted beacon's trail, this remote system had become a hub of covert Khurzan activity away from prying eyes. Valra scanned the surface, searching for signs of settlement where the radicals may have set up a base.

"There, in the northern latitudes, evidence of structures and excavation," observed Zajid, adjusting the long-range sensors. Valra spotted the same pattern: what looked to be bunkers and tunnels spread across an arid plateau. A hypertension complex extended deep underground.

"It appears we have found the source...yet we must be cautious," Valra replied. Further scans showed a sprawling above-ground camp filled with vessels and temporary shelters. This was no mere splinter cell, but a planet-wide network.

"We should land covertly and attempt to infiltrate the bunker levels," Zajid suggested, bristling at the presence of so many extremists. "I know their tongue and can extract information."

Valra hesitated, weighing the risks. Drawing closer could expose them, yet more knowledge was needed if they were to undermine this vile enterprise. She nodded finally. "Agreed, but stay close my friend. Khurzan's web ensnares subtly."

Zajid plotted an approach vector avoiding sentinel ships on patrol in the upper atmosphere. Their sleek cloaked ship slipped down through the red mists shrouding the planet's surface. In the distance, the lights of massive encampments flickered ominously against the nightside curve of the planet. What hatred simmered down there, waiting to be unleashed?

Finding an isolated canyon beyond the perimeter of the main base, Zajid brought them down to the planet's surface and activated full stealth systems. They would continue the rest of the way on foot. Valra pulled up her facial wrappings, once again taking the guise of a Khurzan fanatic.

Together, they descended the rocky trails leading toward the central bunker complex looming ahead. The harsh red landscape felt like an alien world compared to the lush capital they knew. What darkness had taken root in such a desiccated place?

A towering sentry post blocked entry to the heart of the sprawling base. Valra's heart pounded, but Zajid spoke the deep code phrases with natural ease. After an agonizing pause, the gates slid open. Phase one was complete; now for the dangerous depths.

Donning stolen access cards, they wound their way downward via narrow tunnels thorough the chromium walls. The angry echoes of guards and workers reverberated all around. Soon they came upon a secured chamber guarded by twin sentries clad in black.

Zajid repeated the entry codes and rituals. They were granted access to a room filled with banks of cryptic electronics as a communication hub. Now they could tap the very heart of Khurzan's web. Valra quickly hacked the control systems while Zajid fended off suspicion.

"Brothers! A wondrous vision came to me...the Divine Fire has chosen this planet as the crucible of change!" Zajid improvised loudly. The guards nodded, transfixed by mystical possibility. Valra continued decoding encrypted data unseen.

Hours passed feverishly as Valra siphoned plans, rosters, financials—anything to trace the outlines of Khurzan's resurgence. The scope of it all left her mind reeling. How had so much been hidden right under the surface?

With the golden glow of dawn seeping down the tunnels, Valra finished her infiltration. She nodded silently to Zajid; they had risked enough. As they ascended toward daylight and escaped, the chambers below seethed with activity. Discovering the breach was only a matter of time.

Valra and Zajid quickened their pace through the winding tunnels, the sounds of activity in the bunker growing louder. Had their infiltration been detected? Valra's heart pounded as they climbed toward the surface exit.

Emerging into the harsh sunlight, they shielded their eyes and made for the canyon where their ship lay hidden. In the distance, patrol ships buzzed through the reddish skies. One broke formation and angled toward their position.

"We may have company soon." Zajid growled, increasing speed. Valra scanned the rocky terrain, looking for any advantage should pursuers appear. Her mind raced through scenarios as the ship came into view.

The patrol ship swooped low over their canyon, scanners sweeping. Valra and Zajid ducked behind boulders, avoiding detection. After several tense moments, the ship moved on. They broke cover and raced to board their cloaked vessel.

"We must take the data we've uncovered back to the capital immediately," Valra urged, vaulting into the pilot's seat. "If Khurzan suspects a breach, they may accelerate their timetable."

Zajid slammed his fist against the hatch control. "First we should vaporize this vile place from orbit!" His protective anger burned hotly. Valra placed a hand on his muscular arm.

"Another day, my friend. Revelation, not destruction, is our way now." Zajid reluctantly nodded, settling into the navigation seat as Valra sent them rocketing skyward.

A proximity alarm sounded as they cleared the canyon. The patrol ship was looping back around, weapons primed. Valra piloted evasively through the rock spires dotting the plateau. "Looks like we've worn out our welcome!"

The Khurzan vessel spewed searing volleys of particle fire. Valra banked sharply, barely evading the barrage. Zajid returned fire with the ship's plasma cannons, striking its engine array. The patrol ship erupted in flames and careened down in a blaze of glory.

Their ship shot upward through the atmosphere. Below, the hidden Khurzan complex receded, though its darkness still stretched far. Valra grimly set course back to the capital. Time was now uncertain.

Wellshire listened gravely as Valra related all she had uncovered in the data cores: Khurzan infiltration points, bombing plans, indoctrination camps. The scope of the threat dwarfed their worst fears.

"You took a great risk, my friends. But revelation brings understanding." Wellshire's form shimmered with contemplation. "We must strategize our response with utmost care."

Valra clenched her fists. "While we wait, terror and confusion reign. There is too much we still don't know." She thought back to the patrolling ships. "How did they consolidate so many resources in secret?"

"The shadows yet conceal their greatest allies..." Zajid scowled.

Wellshire dimmed slightly. "We must remain vigilant." Hope seemed fragile, but Valra knew their cause was just. Somewhere ahead, a new dawn waited.

Chapter 15

The capital sank into fearful unrest following Valra and Zajid's ominous findings. Allegations flew wildly as the Khurzan's hidden hand seeded chaos. Valra despaired finding any clear path forward. Each day the darkness advanced, strangling hopes once so bright.

Late one night as Valra sat alone struggling to see light through the blinding gloom, an unexpected communication came through on the ancient frequency she thought long abandoned. Scrambled visuals flickered to life showing a familiar face from so long ago–Dr. Jessica Middleton of Earth.

"Valra...I pray this message finds its way to you..." Jessica's voice conveyed urgency across the vast gulfs of space. Valra reconfigured the antique receiver, shocked to see her friend after so many cycles apart.

"Dr. Middleton! You should not have risked sending this. But your voice is a balm amidst the storm," Valra replied warmly. Explanations could wait, any lifeline was precious now.

Jessica gave a knowing smile tinged by deep concern in her eyes. "I understand there is darkness rising again in your skies...know you have allies still on Earth should you call for aid."

A stunned silence lingered after the message ended as abruptly as it had arrived. Valra had never thought she would hear from the homeworld again. But Jessica's compassionate wisdom endured. Here was hidden hope.

Wellshire further analyzed the cryptic transmission, tracing its origin to a quarantined moon in Earth's solar system—the same one Jessica had fled to with the stolen Meridian files so long ago. She had known of Valra's plight across the endless divide. But how was yet unclear. There had been no communication between their worlds since the earliest days of reconciliation.

"I believe the answers we seek may dwell there." Valra said. Wellshire's projections rippled thoughtfully as he processed the possibilities. Perhaps buried there were solutions to the darkness now enclosing them.

The three planned in utmost secrecy. If Khurzan discovered even a tenuous link to Earth still existed, they would surely move to sever it. After many cycles apart, Valra would embark on a solitary voyage into the unknown.

Slipping away in a cloaked ship, Valra set course for the star system of Earth, heart pounding. She had not dared imagine returning to humanity's cradle after so long among the stars. What revelations awaited her there? Would old ghosts be awakened by revisiting the past? Valra steeled herself against doubt and plunged onward.

Piercing the Sol system's boundary, Valra was shaken as her ship passed by the swirling blue Earth still lovely as ever. How many generations had passed there since her absence? As Valra approached Europa—Jupiter's frozen, quarantined moon mentioned in Jessica's cryptic message—she prepared to make contact. A massive underwater base on the frozen moon responded to her hail using Meridian encryption methods—a secreted sanctuary here at humanity's doorstep. As Valra's ship passed through shimmering defense shields, she knew any secrets harbored here were ancient indeed. What had Jessica uncovered?

Docking within the stark interior bay, Valra was greeted by a delegation of silent figures clad completely in midnight robes marked with intricate sigils. As they escorted her down gleaming obsidian corridors, Valra was struck by the sheer scale of this place. It had the ambiance of a religious complex.

Her guides led her to an ornate chamber, where a council of robed elders sat in solemn silence. At their center was Jessica—her familiar face now withered by time, yet still sharply intelligent. Her presence suggested this place held more history than Valra realized.

"Valra...we have awaited your return for many generations." Jessica's voice remained compassionate but now resonated with solemnness. Clearly there were revelations to unfold here.

The council listened silently as Valra related the Khurzan resurgence threatening all they had built. She spoke plainly of their desperate need for any knowledge or resources that could help avert disaster. The stakes for both their peoples had never been higher.

When Valra finished her plea for aid, the council stirred quietly. Finally, Jessica spoke. "There are hidden bonds between Earth and your ancestors—secrets we have kept for an age knowing that one day understanding would be needed. That time has come."

Valra's mind reeled at the notion of hidden bonds between humanity and the Ancients. She turned to Jessica, eyes filled with hope and confusion. "I do not understand...how could our pasts be linked?"

Jessica nodded knowingly. "There are truths your people forgot during the ages of exile. But the Order of Meridian has safeguarded ancient knowledge." She entered a series of commands on a glowing pedestal. An expansive hologram flickered to life.

Valra gasped as an intricately marked star chart, spanning the galaxy, was displayed before her. She recognized familiar systems, but they were connected via strange pathways and markers unlike any known space lanes. Jessica zoomed in on one luminous node situated ominously at the convergence of many routes. The Sol system—humanity's cradle.

"You see, your ancestors made contact with worlds beyond long before humanity took root," Jessica intoned gravely. "Earth became a hub for their exploration and trade...a gateway."

Valra's mind spun trying to reconcile this revelation with all she understood. Seeing her confusion, Jessica went on. "We discovered these ancient cartographic relics encoded deep in the Meridian archives. But we lacked the context...until now."

"And you believe these hidden connections to Earth can aid our fight against Khurzan?" Valra asked, sensing there were revelations still to come that would irrevocably reshape her universe.

Jessica nodded solemnly, zooming the star map into a remote, forgotten sector tinged with ominous markers. "Here, near the edge of the Zijkhal Expanse, there is an ancient colony world rich in precursor ruins...and secrets. That is where you will find the power to illuminate Khurzan's shadows."

Valra looked on in wonder at the mysterious path laid out before her. Earth and its children had transcended their isolation. Hope kindled anew for revelations time had obscured but truth would restore. She embraced Jessica in gratitude, knowing a new horizon awaited.

Valra could scarcely process the revelations unfolding before her. To glimpse the Ancients' sprawling civilization spanning the stars in its full glory was overwhelming. So much had been forgotten over the millennia. She turned to Jessica with brimming curiosity.

"Tell me, what other truths about our shared past remain obscured?"

Jessica waved a sweeping hand, summoning a cascade of holographic records and artifacts from ages past. "We pieced together fragments from the impossibly distant eras before history began anew. Oaths bound the Order of Meridian to secrecy, until the right moment arose."

Valra stepped through the swirling projections, enraptured. Sleek ships of unknown design docked with towering orbital complexes. Ancestral Progenitors conversed with primitive societies starting their first steps: Minoans, Akkadians, Olmecs. She recognized her kinsmen's influence in the rise of civilizations now long turned to dust.

Her heart caught glimpsing images of early humans clustered around a landing space craft on an African plain, faces filled with awe and fear. Had the Ancients once walked openly on Earth before humanity's remembering? Endless questions flared in Valra's mind.

Noticing her wonderment, Jessica smiled. "Now you glimpse the vast scope of what came before. But the past offers more than mere history." With a wave of her hand, the holograms vanished as quickly as they had appeared. Jessica's eyes became intent.

"If you follow the path charted through the Zijkhal Expanse, you will find a world rich in technologies left behind after the Ancients' fall. They can aid your mission and reveal the way forward."

Valra's mind turned from past mysteries to the perilous present. Somewhere beyond the Expanse's benighted border lay potential salvation from Khurzan's poisonous schemes. An arduous trial awaited, but she would not falter. The light must prevail.

With Jessica's gift of knowledge, Valra prepared to depart from humanity's hidden sanctuary. Final goodbyes were shared, along with earnest wishes of hope. Before she left, Jessica pressed a small object into Valra's palm, an ancient sigil ring imprinted with intricate symbols.

"This was once given to your ancestors in trust...to be returned when the day of truth dawned. May it shield you on the journey ahead."

Valra closed her fingers around the ring, feeling suddenly connected by an unbroken chain to all who had come before. She embraced her friend one last time and turned to depart into the stars once more. A destiny awaited light years away. But she would not walk the path alone.

Valra's sleek ship leaped into endless night, traversing the fathomless gulfs between stars. Jessica's revelations still astonished, but focus was needed for the dangerous path ahead. Valra studied the ancient sigil ring gifted to her at departure. The intricately woven metallic bands shifted colors as they caught the light. Markings like circuitry laced its surface, hinting at untold complexity within. What secrets did it hold?

As she continued her journey, Valra noticed the ring grow subtly warm against her skin whenever she used her psychic abilities to interface with the ship. Curious, she extended her consciousness through the glittering band, probing delicately. A reservoir of immense energy became detectable just beyond her inner sight's reach. This was no mere trinket, but a tool of power.

Testing cautiously, Valra channeled the ring's vibrant energy while piloting the ship through a shimmering gamma nebula. Response became instantaneous and exhilarating. Space-time distortions rippled ahead of her, revealing hidden currents and obstacles. A conduit to forces beyond her natural gifts had awakened. The Ancients' science was incomparable.

Approaching the Expanse's benighted boundary, Valra relied on the ring's protective vibrations to shield her from disorientation. The tenebrous barrier wavered before the alloy's resonance, allowing safe passage through. Guided by her enhanced senses, Valra plunged into the uncharted darkness, undaunted by the perils ahead. The ring would light her way.

After many cycles traversing the perilous Expanse, Valra traced the path to the specified colony world. An azure gas giant loomed ahead marked with the glyphs shown on Jessica's star-map. In close orbit spun an ashen, cratered sphere wreathed in wispy clouds—her destination.

As Valra approached cautiously, sensors revealed a blighted landscape marred by violent upheavals with nothing organic surviving on the surface. Yet below the radiation-scoured wastelands were intricate subterranean structures and power sources of extraordinary scale. What had Jessica hoped she would find here?

Valra landed her ship near the largest underground complex, using the ring's protective aura to shield herself from harsh conditions outside. She donned an environment suit and disembarked, tools at the ready. At the entrance marked on her star chart, she found rows of intricate logic-crystal locks barring access. The ring at her hand glowed in resonance, and the portal slid open.

Descending through silent crystalline corridors, Valra reached a vast central chamber housing alien equipment of startling sophistication. Stasis fields contained antimatter reactors, matter compilers, and fractal consciousness cores—technologies of God-like power. With these, she could reshape reality itself to defeat Khurzan. The Ancients' legacy would save the future.

Deeper in the vaults, Valra discovered suspended animation chambers still active after eons. They held the last survivors of a forgotten civilizational zenith which perished battling forces that nearly consumed the galaxy. They were the Premier Ones, spoken of only in scattered myths, and their knowledge was exceptional.

At the center of the stasis hall stood an honor guard, clad in ornate armor forged from pure carbon nanotubes. They stirred to life and spoke in a musical language as the ring granted Valra access. "The awakening is upon us. We shall aid your quest." Hope had survived deathless—a new dawn was imminent.

Valra could scarcely believe what the ancient vaults held. Technologies and lifeforms lost since before her civilization's dawning waited silently below the dead world's irradiated surface. The power lurking here could reshape reality, if wielded rightly. But suspicion flickered in Valra's mind.

"You claim to desire aiding my cause, yet you know not what fury consumes our galaxy now," she addressed the newly roused Premiere Ones guardedly. Their leader, encased in an intricate spherical capsule, responded in soothing tones.

"Rest easy, voyager. Within these vaults all eras convergence. Your conflict is known to us, through currents subtle and profound." Strange multi-hued displays pulsed around the sphere as it spoke. Valra sensed its consciousness was vastly beyond her comprehension.

"If you can see beyond now, tell me true—will we triumph over the darkness rising in our skies?" she asked plainly, steeling herself for bleak prophecy as the ring dimmed on her hand.

A melodic chime sounded from the sphere. "Certainty eludes even our vision. For untold divergences bloom from every act. But your coming was predicted, Valra of the Firstborn."

Valra gasped as her name was spoken, bringing back distant childhood memories of her mother's lullaby tales—fragmented myths of those who came before. Could her people's origins be traced to these Premiers? Had they guided her ancestors eons ago?

Sensing her wonderment, the Premiere opened long-sealed databanks attuned to Valra by the ring's hidden code. Lost records of the Ancients' exodus and forgotten years living shadowed on remote worlds cascaded before her in holographic light. She saw the fear and desperation that haunted her people then...and now as well. But mingled still with hope.

"All that happened prepared your civilization for this crucible. We can guide you back into the light, but decisive action is needed." The Premiere extracted a bulbous crystalline object from an ornate receptacle. This cognitron holds our collective wisdom. Receive it, and see truly.

Valra hesitated, every teaching warning against such fusion of consciousness. Yet she had come too far to falter now. Bracing herself, she took the pulsing cognitron. Wonders and terrors spanned the eons flooded her awareness as it integrated. When she regained focus, her perspective had shattered and reformed.

"Now you behold the weave in full, and our role at its end," the Premiere intoned solemnly. Valra saw with terrible clarity the recurring cycles of destruction that had scattered her ancestors. Khurzan's kind had arisen before under different names but with the same blind hatred. This time must be different.

"Give me the tools to heal our past, so my people may have a future," she pleaded to the gathered Premiers. A silent accord rippled between them. They presented ancient kinetic projectors and quantum wave-guides capable of restructuring matter and minds. Hope flickered anew.

"Stay the course bravely. Where one way closes, fresh beginnings emerge." With those final words resonating within her, Valra departed the vaults carrying the precious instruments. A ruthless cosmic tempest awaited back home, but now she had lightning rods with which to change destiny's course. The cycle would be broken.

Chapter 16

The return voyage through the Zijkhal Expanse left Valra much changed by the revelations and technologies gained from the ancient vaults. Vast gulfs of knowledge bridged eons from past to future now lived within her mind. The full scope of the struggle against Khurzan was laid bare, along with the dim and distant path to victory.

Wellshire and Zajid greeted Valra anxiously when she arrived back home. While she was away, Khurzan provocations had intensified, with blood spilled in clashes between factions. Each night saw flames of hate grow higher. Swift and resolute action was needed before all was consumed.

Valra gathered the Council and detailed what the journey had unveiled: histories forgotten, technologies discovered, and destinies unlocked. Most reacted with skepticism, the concepts too radical for minds shaped by lifetimes of isolation and fear. But Wellshire's projections flashed intently as he processed the revelations.

"If what you say is true, we stand at a fulcrum point beyond which all futures diverge," the sage AI conjectured. "Khurzan moves ruthlessly to ensure their dark vision prevails. We must be equally decisive for the light."

He and Valra soon retreated to a private sanctum where she could demonstrate the ancient devices' potential. Focusing psychic resonance through the cognitron, Valra accessed the lost Premier archives detailing construction of quantum portals. Wellshire grew thoughtful as new possibilities took form.

"With such gateways, we could evacuate populations to secure refuge worlds beyond Khurzan's reach," he mused. The non-lethal applications of the kinetic projectors also intrigued him. Perhaps the technologies Valra brought back could enable resolution without mass destruction.

Later, as Valra sought rest, Zajid confronted her, anger smoldering in his eyes. "While you were away chasing myths, the enemy poisoned hearts and twisted faith! Only decisive confrontation can purge this cancer from our society."

Valra placed a calming hand on his muscular arm. "A warrior's fists cannot slay beliefs, my old friend. But there are new paths shown that I must walk first, before conflict." Unease lingered in Zajid's face, but he grudgingly nodded and took his leave.

That night, Valra stood alone watching the capital's fear and frantic motion from a high tower. Somewhere Khurzan's masters looked to spark an inferno that would consume all. She closed her eyes, feeling the cognitron and ring pulsing in harmony at her core. The power to change destiny was within her grasp at last. It was time.

Valra broadcast her message openly on all channels, reaching every world and faction. "People of the stars, a darkness has risen that only light can answer. I come bearing lost wisdom to guide us safely through the storm."

She continued unveiling the recovered records, quantum technologies, and plans to provide safe harbor for any who sought it, whatever their faith or origin. Gasps rippled across inhabited space as long-buried secrets came to light.

"We stand together at a crossroads. Down one path lies fear, hatred and endless division. But I have seen a new way where hope still speaks. The choice is ours."

As her call echoed through the void, Khurzan's leadership recoiled in fury, their schemes threatened by revelations exposing their distorted history and calls for unity. But many hearts stirred with relief hearing of refuge. Valra had cast the first stone into the dark waters. Ripples would soon spread.

In the cycles following Valra's revelations, factions arose in chaos and realignment. Many sought the sanctuary she offered beyond Khurzan's reach. But the enemy worked ruthlessly to combine power through fear and deception. Wellshire guided construction of quantum sanctuary gates with the Premiere technology, but time was scarce.

Valra stood watch daily as long lines of refugees waited to pass through the shimmering portals, emerging lightyears away on readiness planets. Khurzan insurgents increasingly targeted the gate facilities, but Zajid led security forces to repel them. Valra hoped compassion might still carry the day.

But one night terror struck at the very heart of the capital. A massive starship, bristling with planet-cracking weapons and launching swarms of parasitic drones, emerged from dark space on the city's edge. Annihilation seemed imminent, until Valra intervened.

Focusing intensely through the ring and cognitron, she generated a psychic shield across the entire metropolis, deflecting the incoming firestorm. Citizens watched in awe as explosions rippled across the scintillating barrier. Valra strained furiously to maintain the protective shell as more hammer blows rained down.

From the shielded council spire, Wellshire targeted key systems across the marauder ship with strategic viral attacks, disabling its weapons and parasite delivery systems. Zajid led attacks of fighter ships to draw its fire and evade relentlessly.

After hours of torment, the warship withdrew, damaged and humiliated. Valra collapsed in exhaustion from the tremendous psychic exertion. The capital was safe for now, but it was just the first of surely more brutal assaults to come. Khurzan was moving to end this.

During the attack's aftermath, fearful debates erupted over how to secure the future. Hardliners pushed aggressively for militarization and preemptive strikes. This time Zajid's voice rang among the war-minded.

Valra spoke passionately for continuing refugee evacuation and exploring nonviolent solutions. But each new attack and provocation eroded hopes of reconciliation. She felt the cognitron's wisdom wavering against the primal drive for vengeance. The path was blurring.

Seeking clarity in solitude, Valra retreated to access the Premiere archives from her ship. She found Zajid there waiting. His eyes burned with conviction as he made an urgent appeal.

"This crusade left you wise but weakened. Your gifts saved lives, but more will be lost without strength to defend ourselves. Khurzan knows only force." He lifted an ancient energy blade before her. "Fight alongside me, Valra. Our people need a warrior now."

Valra felt the ring cooling on her hand as she faced him silently. Since childhood they had walked together through darkness and light. But this choice would set their footsteps apart forever. She touched his arm softly, then turned away. There was still hope while she drew breath.

Appearing from her ship, Valra saw the full scale of the growing conflict. Khurzan forces pressed from all sides while refugees continued flocking to the sanctuary gates. Each clash fueled the next in an ever-rising spiral of violence. Time was slipping away.

Valra realized one path remained untested: sharing with Khurzan what she had learned. Perhaps their minds could yet be unlocked from the prison of hate. She would undergo the cognitron convergence process with one of their captured leaders. Understanding could yet be theirs, if she could bear it. The ring flared brightly, and she prepared to depart into the heart of darkness.

Valra embarked on her mission to the remote ice-shrouded space station where the captured Khurzan commander was held captive. Zajid strongly protested attempting dialogue with the fanatical extremist, but Valra hoped contact through the cognitron would create empathy where none existed before.

"Your compassion is your weakness, Valra," Zajid warned ominously as she left. "When it fails, we will stand ready to do what must be done."

Wellshire's expression furrowed with concern as Valra's ship launched. "I have run probability projections of likely outcomes. There is significant risk to you personally in this effort. But potential gains outweigh the trials ahead."

Valra set course resolutely, the ring a steady glow on her finger. "All that has come before leads to this. If we cannot brighten the abyss together, all is surely lost."

The Khurzan commander awaited her arrival with venomous defiance, launching into vicious tirades against her "weakness and corruption." Valra weathered the hatred calmly, preparing the cognitron interface. Finally, she started a psychic linkup.

Instantly the commander's rage melted into shock, and he was overwhelmed as Valra's consciousness mingled with his own. Each experienced the other's life experiences deeply, contextualizing their respective worlds. For long moments their minds were one.

When the link receded, the commander sat in tormented silence as hatred he had nurtured for decades cracked before empathy's light. Valra too now grasped the depths from which Khurzan's cruelty rose. But she also saw the glimmer of his conscience long buried.

"What have I become?" he said at last, agony in his voice. Valra extended a hand in friendship across the chasm. "The person you were before still lives. There are yet miles to walk between us, but we can trace the steps together."

Their dialogue lasted long hours, slowly unraveling decades of fear and demonization. When Valra finally returned to her ship, she allowed herself to feel hope. Perhaps even Khurzan's collective psyche could be turned from the brink through weeks of contact sessions.

But back at the capital, chaotic developments dashed those fragile hopes. While Valra was away, Khurzan initiated a colossal attack, detonating stars along key space routes and obliterating the quantum sanctuary gates and evacuation ships. Millions of lives and any hope of de-escalation were erased in moments.

Enraged, the Council had Zajid launch an overwhelming retaliatory strike on Khurzan's stronghold while Valra was still in transit back. She arrived to find a shaky video of a planet's entire biosphere purified in quantum fire, as Zajid's forces celebrated exterminating the cancer plaguing the galaxy at last.

Valra watched in horror, knowing any fragile trust built with the Khurzan commander was now shattered forever. Zajid approached her, eyes ablaze with conviction. "At last, the enemy knows the taste of vengeance. We will ravage them without mercy until their evil is expunged."

Valra fell to her knees, the ring lifeless and cold, cognitron silenced. She had failed to bring understanding in time. Now the final war beginning would leave no winners, only scorched worlds and broken souls. Dark and light spiraled inward to oblivion. Her quest was over.

Valra sank into despair as all around her descended into blood and chaos. The Chancellor demanded ever more brutal military strikes, spurred on by Zajid's crusading fury. Each fresh atrocity only fueled further retaliation, with no end spiraling in sight.

Valra pleaded desperately for restraint, but moderating voices were drowned out. She even tried to reach Zajid on protected channels, reminding him of their childhood dreams of peace. His only response was cold resolution. "Your time for idealism is past. I will do what must be done."

With each ruthless assault, more of Khurzan's culture was purged. They retaliated by infecting enemy ships with horrific bioweapons, leaving no survivors. Wellshire notified Valra grimly of the rapidly growing casualty projections.

"At current rates of destruction, both civilizations will be functionally extinct within two hundred days. My models offer only one probable path to prevent this."

Valra considered his projection wearily. "And what solution could redeem this madness?" The answer was already sinking in her heart like a stone.

"A weapon using the acquired Premiere technology could irreversibly mutate the neural architecture. It would reinforce each side's xenophobic ideology through meme restructuring. Essentially, end the war by forcefully overwriting hatred and fear."

Valra recoiled in dismay. "I swore never to use those tools for violence, even in hope of peace." Wellshire dimmed pensively. "Then I am out of viable options. Every other projection leads to extinction."

Retreating from the Citadel's blood cries, Valra stared up at passing formations of bombers headed for ruin. She felt the useless ring on her hand, inert since violence took root. Was forced peace through psychic mutation really the only way back from the brink? Or was there some light left to rekindle?

In the cold void, she closed her eyes and focused inward, drawing on near-forgotten exercises from apprenticeship days. As her breathing slowed, flickers stirred deep within. She called on all the wisdom accumulated in her journey: the cognitron's archives, ring's chronicles, guidance from mentors living and gone.

Faint patterns became perceptible in the chaos around her. She honed her senses to their subtleties, shielding against enveloping despair. There, remnants of harmony once woven between factions linger beneath the surface, fragile and undeveloped. They yearned to be known again.

Valra realized with clarity that conquering hate through hate was hopeless. Peace could only grow from small seeds nurtured in secret, as Zajid had nurtured their childhood bond before fear's frost. She would find those rare souls on both sides who were ready to light golden lamps of peace together, unwilling to see darkness triumph. It was time for new pilgrimages of trust.

The Chancellor tried dismissing Valra's initiatives to contact dissidents as futile but relented to avoid provoking her supporters. Valra soon set out on her mission, the ring warming faintly as hope kindled again within. Light still called where wisdom guided.

Chapter 17

Valra navigated the cold void between worlds, relying on the faintest psychic whispers to guide her steps. Somewhere in the scarred battle zones ahead, isolated pockets yearned for concord amid the senseless carnage. She need only send out feelers to resonate with their faint light.

Wellshire tracked Valra's course from afar, ready to alert her of dangers. He no longer tried dissuading her quest, sensing she followed the only path left alive in her heart. "Your strength was never in force, but faith. Let it light your way," were his parting words.

Zaida watched Valra's ship depart from the command deck, jaw clenched. How could she still resist defending their people with righteous fury? Every lost ship was blood on Valra's hands. When Valra's pleas failed as was inevitable, retribution would fall swift and true. None would be left to light fresh fires.

Valra's ring pulsed brighter as she crossed into contested space. On a ravaged moon, sensors showed traces of activity—refugees hiding from endless cycles of violence. She landed her ship and ventured out into the blasted wastelands.

Before long, Valra detected life signals from a camouflaged bunker carved into a canyon wall. Approaching slowly with hands raised, she called out. "I mean no harm. I seek only those willing to rebuild our shared peace."

After tense moments, the concealed door cracked open. Ragged, hollow-eyed civilians appeared, wary but desperate. They represented both factions, sheltering together. Valra's eyes filled with tears. Here was fragile hope worth cultivating.

As she was guided inside, Valra learned these survivors had known cooperation before the poisonous ideologies took hold. Some still believed reconciliation was possible. She shared her own journeys to Earth and the Premiere vaults.

"Beyond the stars, we are all one," she told them. "Hatred ends where wisdom begins. Will you help me plant seeds between our peoples, so that future shades may know harmony?"

The refugees were hesitant but entranced by Valra's words. One scarred old woman stepped forward. "My life has shown we cannot defeat darkness with more darkness. Lead us and let our journey open hearts sealed shut by pain."

They prayed and broke bread together, kindling lights to guide the way. By departure, Valra had coordinates for more prospective oases. Her quiet pilgrimage was underway. However slim the chances, she would help concord take root until its branches could shelter all.

On remote outposts and ships marooned for ages, Valra's gentle persuasion spoke. One by one, the weary and heartbroken released old grudges to grasp fragile new beginnings.

With each world Valra touched, Wellshire tracked a slight decrease in hostilities and casualties overall. Her actions were an insignificant counterforce on an apocalyptic scale. And yet, where no hope stirs, darkness goes unchallenged. She was changing fate's trajectory one conscience at a time.

Word of Valra's pilgrimage spread discretely between worlds. In the shadows of space stations and shelters, her name became a whispered myth. Some claimed she was a ghostly envoy of the lost Ancients, returned to walk the razor's edge between endless war and uneasy reconciliation. Others dismissed the stories as fanciful lies offering false hope. But a few felt called to action by the tales.

On a remote ice planet, Valra was led down into glowing catacombs where geo-thermal vents kept subterranean oceans liquid. There, an unexpected gathering awaited. Representatives had come in secret from the inner systems of both interstellar nations. All were exhausted by endless vengeance, ready to accept any flicker of hope.

Moved by Valra's accounts of her journey, the assembled diplomats and warriors chose to lay down old grudges and forge a confession of peace. The first olive branch extended between factions in decades. Its words flowed from hearts given hope and healing perspective by Valra's testimony.

"We once orbited the same stars, bound by common dreams before time's nebulas clouded memory. Now storm winds gather our tears. We pledge here, whatever past divisions, to guide life's fragile vessel together. May this covenant grow roots till its branches shelter every child of the skies."

Transmitting the confession securely, Valra included Zajid among the recipients. He did not respond, but she knew seeds were being planted in even the most barren soil. What fruit they may yet bear against the whirlwinds none could foresee. But she would nurture concord where she could.

Wellshire monitored Zajid's forces as they continued scouring contested sectors for enemies to destroy. But the quantum fire in their eyes seemed to be dimming since Valra's journey began. Between battles, veiled chatter hinted at growing unease with the unending violence tearing civilizations apart.

"This crusade was righteous once, but its fury consumes all now," one veteran pilot transmitted from his scorched cockpit. "What honor remains in exterminating innocents? I feel only shame."

Observing this, Wellshire opened long unused communication channels. "The first step is taken. When you are ready, I will be waiting." No replies came yet, but the sage AI was patient. Minds unmake slowly what conviction wove tight. But he had helped steer Zajid from darkness before. Perhaps again, given time.

Meanwhile, Valra felt her psychic reserves depleting rapidly. The relays between discordant souls left no time for rest. Each reconciliation kindled new strength within her, but still the war raged fiercely. She focused on the teachings from Earth and the lost Ancients, drawing wisdom for the trials ahead.

As Valra's pilgrimage continued, she found reservoirs of compassion running dry on many worlds. Decades of violence had desensitized entire generations. Hearts once receptive to conciliation were now walled off by bitterness and despair.

On a radiation-scorched planet, Valra addressed a somber enclave digging mass graves for fresh attack casualties. Her stories of rediscovering humanity's lost unity on Earth stirred no resonance here.

"Your words hold no substance for us," their leader said bitterly, turning away. "Sow your fragile seeds elsewhere. Only the wrathful survive this soil."

The rejection weighed heavily on Valra as she departed the grim place. Doubts arose. Had she set out on this journey too late? Was reconciliation merely a faded dream from younger days drowned out by cascading horrors?

Resting at a quiet waystation, Valra meditated and delved into chronicles of how Earth's nations rose above ancient cycles of blood vengeance. Healing took hold only when courageous few listened within for wisdom's whisper through the storms. The Silence passage was often overlooked. She must trust patience.

Arriving at a refugee sanctuary station, Valra was greeted by an old mentor from her apprentice days, a serene mystic named Zalunas. He had tended this haven alone for years, keeping a single candle lit for any seeking solace. Valra felt her inner light rekindling in his presence.

"The war's Great Wheel turns still, but your steps determine its revolutions," Zalunas counseled. Always seek the melody of harmony amidst the clamor of chaos. For those who truly listen, discord can never completely drown it out." Before leaving, he gave Valra a glass harmony orb resonating with frequencies to calm and center. "When shadows encroach, this will recall you to light within. Be the promise for others you seek."

Aboard her ship, cradling the orb's gentle vibrations, Valra reached again for Zajid on private channels. This time his fury seemed tempered by doubt. Word of Valra's pilgrimage had spread even to his decimated fleets. It gave him pause.

"Old friend, there are always alternatives still untried," she implored him. "We can forge peace together." Zajid's eyes held a glimpse of the trusting boy she once knew before fear's winter froze him. He opened his mouth as if to speak, then thought better and signed off. But she knew him well. Positive change was coming.

Wellshire observed Zajid's forces had stopped pursuing enemies in recent cycles. Instead, they drifted as if lost, no longer crusaders certain in purpose. A silent pivot was at hand. At this crossroad, great destinies would unfold.

A board Zajid's battered command ship, reports filtered in of swiftly deteriorating conditions planet side. With supply chains shredded by years of total war, critical shortages now threatened the population's survival. Medicine, food, fuel all dwindled dangerously. The homefront cries for relief could no longer be ignored.

Zajid watched grimly as riots and hoarding spread in the capital on screens. His people were turning against each other in the depths of desperation. This crusade had taken everything from them—even hope for a future.

He opened Valra's last message, re-reading her earnest words. "It is not too late to change course. Meet with me and let our people's wounds be healed." Everything in him recoiled from accepting such naivete. And yet...they had been friends once, before the stars burned. Could she still know his heart better than he knew himself? The past felt very far away.

At last, Zajid gave the order to return home and reestablish essential supply chains. Let diplomacy and relief efforts continue. The time for blood was over. A tide was receding within him, revealing old shores long submerged. What future might await if they charted new stars together?

Valra received word from Wellshire that Zajid was returning to broker an armistice. She wept in relief, scarcely believing redemption could emerge from so much horror. Now healing could truly begin. She set course to rendezvous with his fleet, new strength rising within her.

But as Zajid's ships reached the inner systems, black ops agents loyal to extremist factions started a desperate gambit. If the crusade ended, their grip on power would be finished. They remotely activated a hidden wormhole, unleashing a torrent of warp drones and neutron bombs through space-time toward the homeworlds. Annihilation threatened once more.

Valra sensed the looming darkness and called on all her gifts to shield the planets in time. She managed to divert the worst impacts before collapsing in agony, blood trickling from her eyes and nose. Millions still perished, and white-hot fury reignited across all factions. Vengeful war cries filled the airwaves. Her pilgrimage seemed to have failed.

But Zajid's fleets had seen Valra sacrifice everything to protect their worlds from the extremists' last insane grasp at power. A vision of future unity flickered for them now. They turned on their doomed commanders with mercy and sealed off the wormhole scourge. Some hope yet endured.

Valra drifted in and out of feverish dreams aboard a medical ship. Vague visions filled her mind: Earth's primal dawn, the Ancients' exodus, and the unifying voice calling her to walk between civilizations teetering on the abyss's edge once again.. Each flicker of love and trust had kept cosmic dark at bay, if only for fleeting moments. But the next steps remained clouded.

Wellshire projected reassurance as she recovered. "Rest now. Turning tides move slow but steady." Valra took solace knowing Zajid was safely leading the fleet home. The last desperate ploys of warmongers had failed to derail reconciliation.

But fresh trials awaited Zajid on arrival. The Chancellor was ready to crush any truce and continue the crusade with increasingly lethal planet-scouring weapons. Wild-eyed hordes shrieked for vengeance at rallies, drowning calls for dialogue. Police clashed fiercely with rioters. Chaos reigned in all spheres.

Zajid's officers urged violent suppression of all dissenters. "These traitors threaten everything we have bled for! They must be purified." Zajid's jaw clenched. Once he would have readily complied. But wisdom now tempered might. Valra's light still shone on him from afar.

"I will address them directly. Stand ready." Zajid descended to the podium before the seething crowds and hesitant security forces. The Chancellor bellowed that he was a traitor against all they held sacred. Zajid stood firm.

"Each of you has lost, as I have lost," Zajid began solemnly. "We sought to protect our people, but let rage guide us astray. No victory justifies what these wars have cost our nation's soul."

He continued carefully, neither condemning nor condoning past actions. "Now we stand on oblivion's edge where shadows reign. But light always returns. Will we turn toward it together?" None interrupted as he concluded. "I believe we can."

In the heavy silence, a child emerged with tears streaking dusty cheeks and placed her hand in Zajid's gauntleted fist. Then a widow bearing grief's scars. One by one the crowd approached, wounds unspoken but acknowledged. Light's roots held fast.

The Chancellor fled his failed coup, screaming curses. But order prevailed as Zajid directed relief efforts. Reconciliation was still fragile, but the survivor's will shone stronger. Unmake minds slow what fear and hate once forged firm. But those who were silent heard wisdom's call.

Valra observed all from her infirmary bed, her own trials now secondary. Zajid had faced the darkness within and chosen peace. The most crucial steps were taken. When strength returned, they would walk the path together again at last. Healing could truly begin.

Chapter 18

As Valra's strength gradually returned, tentative preparations began for an unprecedented unity summit between former enemy states. Wellshire helped Zajid in carefully laying diplomatic groundwork to ensure the best chance of success.

But decades of hostility left many factions deeply skeptical, with zealots actively sabotaging reconciliation efforts however they could. Security concerns were paramount, with each side fearing the summit could be a pretext for violent treachery.

Valra urged choosing a neutral sanctuary location for the gathering. The two former foes had never before come face-to-face outside theaters of war. Each side must feel safe and heard for progress to unfold.

After arduous debate, an isolated rogue planet was selected, its habitation domes and event halls to host delegations in separate quarters. Distrustful militaries would provide joint security, with Wellshire coordinating intelligence oversight.

The summit would allow representative voices from across societies to speak and be seen, ideally planting seeds of understanding. But so much pain and suspicion burdened the space between them. Valra knew the greatest test still lay ahead.

As guests gathered from lightyears away, Valra meditated daily to prepare her mind and spirit. Profound healing might be possible if old traumas were addressed collectively, unhardening hearts entombed by loss. But carefully tending the fragile trust was supreme.

At last, the opening day arrived, as once implacable foes' shuttles descended through wispy clouds surrounding the planet. The cities below had been designed eons ago for peaceful exchange and contemplation before the Divide. Perhaps such vision could be rekindled here.

Valra waited in the central forum with Zajid, Wellshire, and the principal envoys. When the former adversaries entered, all was silent except for the sound of footsteps reverberating off marble walls and vaulted ceilings. Long suppressed pain filled the air.

The chief delegates halted at a distance, silently beholding faces they had only seen through targeting scopes and propaganda. Then Valra stepped forward. "From hope we come, and to peace we return. Shall we walk the way together?"

No words could encompass the moment. But one envoy offered her hand, then the other. None withdrew. Something shifted delicately. The effects of the peaceful gesture had begun to ripple outward. The summit's opening ceremonies proceeded solemnly, with each side's history recounted both in glory and shame. None denied misdeeds or absolved guilt. All who had suffered were honored. Then pensive silence enveloped the hall as participants contemplated the cascading tragedies born of division.

After days of secluded private reconciliation sessions, the delegations at last convened in the central forum. Valra opened the floor for delegates to speak their hearts' truths. Pent-up grief and rage spilled forth as many relived haunting memories of loss.

Zajid listened stoically as survivors accused his military of atrocities that shattered families and homes. When given the opportunity, he confessed sins long justified in wartime conscience.

"No orders or beliefs absolve the suffering inflicted by my hands. I can only strive now for reparative justice and guard your people alongside mine." Some wept at his words. Others turned away, nursing enduring distrust. The path was long.

When former enemies aired hostile intentions or bitter condemnations, Valra intervened gently. "From this sacred space, see each other's light beneath the shadows cast. Mercy first for self, then others." Slowly the room calmed. No easy miracles came, but they had witnessed truth.

Small groups were soon meeting daily between sessions, impromptu dialogues kindling. Hesitant sharing of food, music and customs gradually harmonized foes known previously only in battle. Laughter even cautiously sounded at times.

But late one evening, grave news arrived. A renegade faction had attacked defenseless civilian targets along the border on both sides. Outrage exploded instantly, old reflexes stirring violent reprisal. The summit teetered dangerously.

Valra called for patience and faith in their shared bonds. Zajid urgently conferred with commanders to contain militaristic retaliation. Wellshire investigated covertly. For endless hours, the forum abided anxiously.

Wellshire finally reported the self-destructing renegades were fringe radicals acting independently. They intended to reignite mutual hatred, but their evil could not prevail if the delegates held to wisdom. Valra exhorted them gently.

"Those who lit this fire meant to blind us anew but have only purified our vision. With open hearts, let us distinguish light from shadow. Our dead still call to us for hope."

None withdrew after the attack. All only reaffirmed themselves to reconciliation with greater conviction. The renegades' hatred met only compassion, dissipating like vapor. Valra knew from Earth's chronicles that this was the turning point they needed. The worst was behind them now.

Former foes embraced freely, exchanging promises and forgiveness. Each would devote their life to spreading the summit's healing. At the farewell meal, Zajid stood with glass raised.

"From broken shale, living waters spring. Go forth renewed, stewards of peace."

After the summit, ripples of change spread slowly but steadily across worlds scarred by generational warfare. One heart at a time, old prejudices began dissolving as people chose to see their common hopes and needs rather than old divisions.

At Zajid's encouragement, the military pivoted resources towards rebuilding critical infrastructure and services reduced to shambles after decades of fighting. Food, medicine, energy—basic essentials flowed again, relieving much suffering planet side.

Wellshire guided massive reconstruction efforts, drawing on vast databases to improve renewal of urban centers and agriculture. "Your peoples have endured darkness but kept their spirit shining. Now our shared future brightens."

Valra traveled extensively, speaking to gatherings large and small about her journeys to Earth and beyond. She encouraged all to look inward as well as outward, nurturing compassion for self and others. A new generation was rising that could grow up knowing only peace.

But of course, many remnants of the old regimes resisted the changing tide. Ultra-nationalist groups staged rallies and issued fear propaganda, trying to reignite divisions. Small terror cells launched attacks looking to provoke overreactions.

Zajid responded firmly but proportionally to safeguard order and stability. Wellshire helped develop effective strategic deterrence. Valra urged people to react with wisdom rather than reflexive fear and demonization.

At a rally where agitators spewed xenophobic conspiracy theories, one elder woman simply sat cross-legged in front of them. When accosted violently, she did not withdraw or retaliate. Inspired by her courage, others joined in quiet meditation. Soon the hateful chants gave way to introspection. The agitators' anger burned out, their bitterness answered with compassion.

At a naval academy, former enemy trainees undertook joint exercises, bonding quickly through shared challenges. One cadet noted, "In another life we may have fired on each other. Now we are brothers and sisters under the stars."

Even some former hardliners had profound changes of heart after experiencing reconciliation. One ex-commander confessed his past passion. "I was deaf and blind, consumed by self-righteous fury. But mercy allowed me to be reborn."

Two years after the summit, a unity celebration was held at the historic grounds. There Zajid and the other principal envoys stood together without guards between them. Public plazas and fountains where crowds had once clashed violently now saw strangers embracing like old friends.

As fireworks filled the sky that night, Valra let tears of joy fall, knowing this peace would continue widening even long after her days. Planting the first seeds had been her purpose. Now they were mighty trees bearing rich fruit, their sheltering branches reaching ever farther.

Don't miss out!

Visit the website below and you can sign up to receive emails whenever Ken Sandoval publishes a new book. There's no charge and no obligation.

https://books2read.com/r/B-A-MUCV-YYIKF

www.ingramcontent.com/pod-product-compliance
Lightning Source LLC
Chambersburg PA
CBHW020954160726
47994CB00006B/2225